Also by Stuart Kaminsky:

Inspector Porfiry Rostnikov Mysteries

DEATH OF A DISSIDENT

BLACK KNIGHT IN RED SQUARE

RED CHAMELEON

A FINE RED RAIN

An Inspector Porfiry Rostnikov Mystery

Stuart M. Kaminsky

IVY BOOKS • NEW YORK

Ivy Books
Published by Ballantine Books
Copyright © 1987 by Stuart Kaminsky

This is a work of fiction. Names, characters, places and incidents either are the product of the author's imagination or are used fictitiously. Any resemblance to actual events or persons, living or dead, is entirely coincidental.

Library of Congress Catalog Card Number: 86-31549

ISBN - 0-8041-0279-1

This edition published by arrangement with Charles Scribner's Sons

Manufactured in the United States of America

First Ballantine Books Edition: May 1988

To
JESSIE, ALICE, AND LEONARD MALTIN

Think carefully of the town we have seen in the play. Everybody agrees that there is no such town in Russia. But what if it were the town of our soul, lying within each of us?

—Nikolai Gogol, *The Denouement of the Inspector General*

ONE

The MAN SITTING ON GOGOL'S SHOULDERS WAS WEEPing and shouting, but Porfiry Petrovich Rostnikov couldn't hear him. Rostnikov stood in Arbat Square across Gogol Boulevard, straining to hear the man's words over the gentle *bump-thump* of the light September rain. It was very early on a Monday morning. Buses and cars crept up Suvorov Boulevard. People on their way to work on Arbat Street and on the New Arbat—or Kalinin Prospekt, as it was officially known—climbed off the buses or hurried out of the underground Arbatskaya Metro Station behind Rostnikov.

A few people, like Rostnikov, paused to watch the ranting man and wonder how he had climbed the statue, which stood tall and apparently unclimbable in the small park. People pressed their faces against the windows of the buses to catch a glimpse of the man on Gogol's shoulders. A Volga stopped and the bespectacled driver stepped out, cupped his right hand over his eyes, squinted at the man and Gogol, and got back in shaking his head.

"Gogol looks amused, like it's a game," said an old man clutching a cloth bag. He had spoken to Rostnikov, who

1

grunted in reply. Gogol did look amused. There was a small smile on the statue's face, and the man who clung to it had his arms wrapped around the statue's eyes so that it looked as if Gogol were trying to guess who the man might be.

"Gogol liked games," the old man said.

Rostnikov grunted and looked around for a uniformed MVD police officer. Had he not made a routine stop to check on the possible sighting of a known pickpocket, Rostnikov would not now be standing in the rain. He looked again for a uniformed officer. Usually they were quite visible. Moscow is the center of the MVD, the national police responsible for minor law enforcement, initial crime inquiry, traffic, and drunks who climb public statues.

Rostnikov's left leg began to ache and he knew that he should get out of the rain. The leg had been injured when Rostnikov was a fifteen-year-old boy fighting the Germans outside Rostov. He had been labeled a hero then, had been made a policeman—one of the youngest policemen in the Soviet Union—despite his handicapped leg, had been honored with medals that made his father proud and his mother weep. Rostnikov had married, had fathered a son, had been promoted to inspector in the Procurator General's Office in Moscow. The Procurator General, appointed for seven-year terms, the longest term of any Soviet official, was responsible for sanctioning arrests, supervising investigations, execution of sentences, and supervision of trials. As an inspector in the office of the Procurator General, Porfiry Petrovich Rostnikov had earned a reputation as a determined, intelligent investigator. But that was all in the past.

Rostnikov had recently been transferred "on temporary but open-ended duty" to the MVD—the police, uniformed and ununiformed, who directed traffic, faced the public, and were the front line of defense against crime and for maintenance of order. It was clearly a demotion for Rostnikov's too-frequent clashes with the Komityet Gospudarstvennoy Besapasnosti, the State Security Agency, the KGB. It wasn't that Rostnikov was a troublemaker. Far from it. It was simply a matter of the KGB's being involved in so much that it was difficult to avoid them.

Rostnikov was now assigned to central MVD headquarters, serving directly under Colonel Snitkonoy, the Gray Wolfhound. Rostnikov's job was to handle assignments from the Wolfhound on less-than-important cases. After the investigations, if the *doznaniye*, or inquiry, indicated it, the cases might be turned over to the Procurator's Office for further investigation and prosecution, provided, of course, that the KGB did not label the cases political. Since the KGB could label as political everything from sabotage to driving over the thirty-five-mile-per-hour speed limit, every investigation had to be cleared with the KGB. Still, important cases of theft, robbery, and murder usually went to the Procurator's Office. Until August, Rostnikov had been a chief inspector in that office, pursuing the investigations of such important cases.

At the moment, however, Rostnikov was getting wet as he engaged in a literary debate with an old man.

"Jews and cossacks," the old man next to Rostnikov said with a smile. The old man wore a soggy workman's cap and a faded gray jacket. A soppy cigarette that had long ago been stilled by the rain still sat in the corner of his mouth. "Gogol was obsessed with Jews and cossacks," the man explained.

"He was a Ukrainian," said Rostnikov, straining to hear what the man who had now climbed onto Gogol's head was shouting. It was probably Rostnikov's responsibility to try to get the man down. It was a responsibility he preferred to deal with only if no other solution could be found. He had faced drunks and madmen throughout his career. It was always a disaster. Now, at fifty-five, Porfiry Petrovich wanted no more disasters. What he wanted was a young uniformed MVD officer or two who would gain valuable experience from dealing with this ranter and the traffic jam he was creating.

"Gogol was greater than Pushkin," challenged the old man at Rostnikov's side. "You know that."

The crowd under Gogol's statue was growing and would soon spill into the street, tying up traffic.

"Pushkin praised Gogol's depth of feeling and poetry. Tolstoy called Gogol a genius," said Rostnikov.

"I'm not questioning his genius," insisted the old man. "Who's questioning the genius of Gogol? Did I question his genius?" the old man asked. "What I said was—"

"Who is a genius?" interrupted a portly, well-dressed woman with a little mesh bag full of vegetables. "That one's a genius?" She nodded at the ranting man perched on the statue.

"We're not talking about him," corrected the old man. "We're talking about Gogol."

"Of course he was a genius," said the woman. "Who said he wasn't?"

The old man pointed at Rostnikov. "He did."

Rostnikov made up his mind and sighed. "I'm a policeman," he said.

"Then that's different," said the old man, walking in one direction while the well-dressed woman with the vegetables headed toward the metro station.

The word *fly* came wailing from the man on the statue through the sound of gentle morning rain, heavy traffic, and the gathering curious. Rostnikov watched a young uniformed MVD officer push his way through the small, but growing, crowd. If the rain were to stop, the crowd would become a circus. The young policeman called out something official sounding to the man on Gogol's head, but the man laughed. The police officer looked confused, and someone called advice from the crowd. Rostnikov sighed and trudged across the square and Gogol Boulevard, holding out his hand to stop an advancing Moscova sedan that seemed determined to roll over him. At the fringe of the crowd, in spite of the rain, an enterprising man with a sad face badly needing a shave had set up a makeshift fold-out stand and was selling, or trying to sell, vegetable seeds.

"Five for a kopeck," he shouted. "All from Africa. They'll grow as big as your fist."

Business was bad, but not terrible. A family—man,

woman, and two young boys—that seemed to be from the country began to talk to the seed salesman without taking their eyes off the man on the statue. Rostnikov lumbered past them and made his way through the crowd.

"Don't shove," said a young man with long hair. He was wearing American jeans and holding the hand of an equally young girl with practically no breasts who was also wearing jeans—and a white T-shirt that had "The Police" written on it in English. Rostnikov momentarily pondered the meaning of the message. Was it in support of the police? A subtle challenge? Why was it in English?

The rain had slowed, but not stopped, as Rostnikov pushed through the front row of the crowd and heard the police officer shout up at the man blasphemously atop Gogol, "You are disrupting traffic and failing to display proper respect to a national monument. Come down now."

The man moved down to sit on Gogol's shoulders and hugged Gogol's neck and laughed at the sky and the rain.

"Come down?" he shouted, the rain dripping down his dark face. "I can fly down. I flew up here and I can fly down. I am a flyer."

Rostnikov examined the man above him. He seemed familiar, not familiar like a friend, or even like the driver of a bus one sees over and over, but like a face one has encountered, examined. He was in his forties, wearing neat, wet-dark pants, a heavy gray shirt, and a jacket that almost matched the pants. He was well built, like an athlete. He seemed to have some secret that he shared only with the sky and the ear of the statue, which he leaned over to whisper into.

"Officer . . ." Rostnikov said to the policeman.

He responded, "Back, stay back."

"I'm Inspector Rostnikov," Rostnikov explained, wiping rain from his brow.

The police officer turned quickly, came to attention, and then relaxed openly, pleased to have a superior take over a situation that was beyond him. The officer, hardly more than a boy, had reddish cheeks and a pouty lower lip.

"Yes, Comrade Rostnikov, I recognize you," he said. "This man . . ."

"Officer?"

"Timis Korostyava," the officer said.

"Korostyava," Rostnikov said, looking up at the man above them, "get some help and move the crowd back. Tell them they'll be late for work. I'll deal with the man who flies on statues."

"Yes, Comrade," Korostyava said with a relieved smile as he turned with great zeal to order the reluctant crowd back. The crowd argued, Korostyava insisted, and as far as Rostnikov could tell, the policeman did an adequate job. From the corner of his eye, Rostnikov saw two more uniformed officers making their way down the sidewalk. The crowd seemed to have grown to more than a hundred as Rostnikov took another step toward Gogol.

"I am Inspector Rostnikov," Rostnikov called up to the man.

"*Gospodin*, Comrade," the man called down with a smile. Then the smile turned to a frown. "I don't care who you are. I am here to talk to Gogol, to cheer him up, to ask his advice."

"Then," said Rostnikov, "you have chosen the wrong Gogol. The one you are on is the smiling Gogol, the standing Gogol. He was put here in 1952 after the war to replace the seated, sad Gogol. The Gogol you want is down there." Rostnikov pointed over his shoulder down Suvorov Boulevard. "Just on the other side of the underpass," he continued, "in the courtyard on the left, number 7a Suvorov Boulevard, right in front of the house where Gogol lived in Moscow, where he wrote. You can't see him from the street. Why don't you come down and we'll go talk to him, cheer him up?"

The man leaned forward, almost falling. From the crowd behind him Rostnikov heard a woman gasp in fear, anticipation of tragedy.

"You hear that, Nikolai?" the man whispered loudly into the statue's ear. "This fire hydrant of a policeman who knows so much thinks I should abandon you."

The man leaned dangerously forward to examine the face of the statue and then sat back again.

"Gogol is amused," he announced.

"I was a young policeman when this statue went up," Rostnikov explained. "I helped to keep traffic back then as the young men behind me are doing now. It was even raining that morning."

"History repeats itself," the man said, shaking his head wisely.

"As Marx said," Rostnikov continued. "Where I now stand and you sit once stood the walls of the White City. This is where the Arbat Gate stood and where in 1812 Napoleon's army entered the city, set up their cannons, and destroyed the Troitskaya Gate of the Kremlin."

"The 1812 Overture?" asked the man, letting go with one hand to clean his face of rain.

Rostnikov wasn't sure, but he nodded.

"You know history," the man on the statue said.

"Some," agreed Rostnikov conversationally.

"Can I ask you something, policeman who knows history?" the man said in a loud whisper no more than fifty or sixty people in the crowd behind Rostnikov could hear. Rostnikov nodded for the man to ask. Again he had the feeling that he had seen this man, even that the man looked appropriate clinging to the statue.

"What's a man to do? He works. His whole life he works until he can fly. And then he discovers that he can fly over the city, over the country, over the ocean. Would you like to fly over an ocean, Comrade Rostov?"

"Rostnikov," Rostnikov corrected. "Yes, I would like to fly," he said, thinking of his own failed attempts to get out of the country with his wife, Sarah. "But I have a bad leg and I am too old to fly. You need a special passport, special papers, to fly."

"No, you don't," the man said, leaning dangerously forward. He held the pointing finger of his right hand up to his lips to indicate that he was about to tell a secret. His lone, clutching hand almost failed him, but he balanced expertly and didn't fall. A smattering of applause from the crowd drew a small smile and a nod of the head from the man on the statue.

"I could tell you how to fly if you had property, money, not Soviet money, but money from the dirty"—the man spat into the wind and rain at the thought—"countries."

"I would like to have you tell me," said Rostnikov. "But look," he turned and pointed at the crowd, at the traffic, "you are stopping people from going to work. I'm standing here soaking. I have only two suits and can't afford to lose one to the weather. I'm not such a young man and I have a leg—"

"What do you take me for, a fool? May your father choke on half-cooked jelly if you take me for a fool," the man said, and then, loudly to the crowd, "He takes me for a fool."

"Don't take him for a fool," a young male voice called out, followed by a ripple of laughter.

"You're not a fool," Rostnikov said gently. "You are a little drunk, a little confused, a little unhappy, a—"

"Of course I am!" cried the man. "I'm a Russian. But the important question is, Do you like me?"

"At the moment." Rostnikov sighed. "But I will probably begin to grow impatient and have to call in a truck and ladder."

"If you do," the man announced, "I will simply fly from here." With this he let go with both hands, and Rostnikov leaped forward awkwardly to try to anticipate and possibly break his fall. But the man didn't fall. He clung to the neck of the statue with his feet, leaned backward, and then sat up, arms out, dripping with rain, as the crowd applauded.

Rostnikov turned, found Korostyava, and beckoned for him to come forward. The young officer came at a run, his black boots splashing in puddles.

"You and the others clear the area, break up the crowd," he whispered. "This man is playing to them. He might even jump."

Korostyava nodded, turned, and hurried toward his fellow officers to begin clearing the street if they could.

"What's your name, Comrade?" Rostnikov called up to

the man, who watched as the police started to disperse the crowd behind Rostnikov.

"What? My name? Duznetzov, Valerian Duznetzov."

"Duznetzov, what do you do when you are not tying up traffic and whispering to statues?"

"I told you," Duznetzov said. "I fly. I leap. I fly. I bend. I spring. And sometimes, when I can, I drink. Gogol is not answering. You are not helping. It is time for me to fly."

The man began to rise. Keeping his balance with one hand, and in spite of a definite drunken swaying, he managed to stand on the shoulders of the statue. A good wind would send him tumbling backward. In the street a bus or car driver hit a horn, though it was prohibited by law inside the city. Duznetzov touched his forehead in salute to the warning horn and looked down at Rostnikov. The rain had begun to fall harder, sending a chill through Rostnikov, a familiar ache through his leg.

"Why are you doing this, Duznetzov?" Rostnikov asked.

"Because I can neither go nor stay. It's very simple. They give me no choice. They never did."

"They?" shouted Rostnikov. "Who are they?"

"One is the man who sees thunder." Duznetzov laughed as he spoke into the falling rain. "My body can fly but my soul is weak. I shall miss vodka and ice cream, Rostnikov. It would be better if the sun were out. I think I could like you."

"Perhaps we could be friends?" Rostnikov suggested.

"Too late," said Duznetzov with a shrug. "I should have shaved."

Rostnikov was never sure whether it was a gust of wind or a determined leap that sent Duznetzov into a midair somersault off Gogol. Screams cut through the rain behind Rostnikov, who hurled himself forward in a useless attempt to get below Duznetzov, to possibly catch him, cushion his fall. Even with two good legs, Rostnikov knew, he could never have made it, but he tried and almost instantly wished he had not. He splashed behind the statue just in time to witness the leaping man land headfirst on the concrete walkway. Rostnikov stopped, closed his eyes. But he closed them too late. He added the image of Duznetzov's crushed skull to a mosaic of terrible memories from the war and years of dealing with victims and madmen.

There was no use now in hurrying to the body. He let the uniformed police run past him, heard their boots hit the walk as he stood forgetting the rain.

"Keep them back," he ordered, and two of the policemen halted. One, the young one who had been first on the scene, looked at the body and then turned and faced Rostnikov. His face was pale, his mouth open.

"Are you going to be sick?" Rostnikov asked softly so the other two officers couldn't hear.

"I don't know," Korostyava said. "I . . . he was just drunk."

"Go. Go take care of the crowd," Rostnikov said, and the young policeman began to walk slowly away from the scene without looking back. "And be sure to write your report and turn it in. Include everything that man said. Everything, even if it made no sense."

Korostyava's back was turned, but he nodded like a drunk about to drop into a stupor.

"He's dead, Comrade Inspector," shouted one of the policeman—an older, heavyset sergeant—at the body.

"Thank you," answered Rostnikov.

The rain suddenly let up. It didn't quite stop, but it ceased applauding madly against the pavement. Rostnikov checked his watch. It was nearly seven and he should have been back at the Petrovka Station for the morning meeting with the Gray Wolfhound's staff. The street had now been reasonably cleared of pedestrians by six or seven police officers. Had it not been raining, Rostnikov was sure, it would have taken at least two dozen to keep the street clear.

"His name is Duznetzov," the older officer at the body shouted to Rostnikov, who forced himself to turn and look at the policeman, who held up a limp wallet. "He's with the circus."

"Not anymore," Rostnikov said, but he said it to himself and to the smiling Gogol.

At the moment Valerian Duznetzov flew into the morning rain, Oleg Pesknoko, who was rumored to have had a Mongol grandmother, dipped his hands in chalk, rubbed them together, and wondered why Duznetzov was late. Pesknoko rubbed his shaved head and took off his warm-up jacket and placed it carefully on the bench. Then Pesknoko adjusted his blue practice tights, rubbed his stomach (telling himself that he would have to lose at least fifteen pounds), and stepped into the small, silent circus ring.

Duznetzov was probably drunk again, thought Pesknoko as he strode across the ring and shivered. He rubbed his shoulders and did a series of limbering-up exercises. Each year the exercises took longer. Each year it became harder to think up new routines, to find ways to justify them to the political committee. Neither he nor Duznetzov was very good at thinking up the routines or at finding some reason why their aerial act fulfilled the conditions of Marxist/Leninist ideology. Oleg was still considered the best catcher in the circus in spite of his fifty-nine years, and Duznetzov was considered the most daring flyer in the business. But Oleg's Katya was the brain. She was the youngest. She was pretty. She could smile and she could fly, perhaps not with the best, but she was good enough when she was backed by Oleg and Valerian. And, Oleg realized without quite admitting it consciously, Katya was the only one of the trio with a brain.

But now, with the new director out looking for young talent, Oleg, Valerian, and Katya would have to work twice as hard, be doubly inventive, if they were to stay with the circus. They had a protector with a vested interest in the act, but even the protector could not guarantee their jobs. And, Oleg thought as he began to climb the rope ladder, it was essential that they not lose their position, not yet, not with the Lithuanian and Latvian trip scheduled for October. No, he thought, coming to the top of the ladder, they would have to do something sensational, something so daring that the new director could not possibly consider replacing them.

Oleg stood on the platform and looked down at the net below him, at the empty, dark corners of the arena. They had talked, the three of them, of what they might have to do if they were unable to secure their place in the troupe. It was a desperate second choice, one that none of them wanted to take, for one could never be sure of the reaction of the Komisol representative if he were told that certain counterrevolutionary transactions were going on in the circus. It wasn't something Oleg wanted to do, but they had decided to consider it. The possibility had sent Duznetzov into a deep gloom. But what could you expect from a flyer, Oleg thought, loosening the rope that held his trapeze. Flyers lived on applause, on their nerves. Catchers had to be strong, unappreciated by all but their fellow professionals. It was the difference between himself and Duznetzov. Valerian needed an audience even to practice. Oleg needed only his own appoval and Katya's admiration.

This morning he had planned to try Katya's idea for the one-legged catch and the flip to a hand-in-hand. Oleg was not sure they could do it. Five years ago he would have felt confident, but their reflexes were not the same. They were, however, highly motivated.

Without Valerian, there was little Oleg could do. He had left Katya sleeping in their apartment, knowing she would come in an hour or two when she awakened and found his note, would come and criticize, advise, encourage. Oleg sighed, checked his hands, grabbed the bar, and swung out over the net below. The rush of freedom he always felt when he swung above the net pulsed through him and made his muscles ripple. He pulled himself up on the swinging bar, forcing himself not to grunt with the effort, and hooked his legs around the bar and the swing ropes. As he swung, he let go of his thoughts, stretched out his arms, imagined the catch, the throw, Valerian's flip, and the split second he would have to grasp the ankle. He swung and imagined. Yes, he decided. He could do it.

Something slipped. He felt or sensed the slip. It was

very slight at first. Oleg was upside down. He seldom looked up to the ceiling; there was no need to do so. But this time he sensed that there was a need. He craned his thick neck up toward the darkness where the ropes were attached. There was someone up there.

"What are you doing?" he called.

The figure continued to maneuver in the darkness, and Oleg definitely felt the trapeze begin to loosen. It made no sense. Oleg would simply release his legs and fall to the net below. He couldn't see who the person working at the ropes was, but he had no doubt that he knew who it was. It could be no one else.

Oleg took one long swing as the trapeze rope began to slip and did a double flip as he released the bar. He hadn't tried a double flip in at least ten years, but he had something to prove to the man above him: that he was capable, that he was not to be frightened, not to be threatened, not to be taken lightly. It was a beautiful double-flip descent that would certainly have brought applause from any audience, but the breaking of the net as he hit it after his thirty-foot drop would have brought gasps of horror. As he struck the net, Oleg understood. The net was not tied down. It was not going to catch him, was not going to break his fall. Just before he struck the blue concrete of the ring floor and broke his neck, Oleg, tangled in netting, was sure that he heard the echo of applause from a solitary figure high above him.

Hours earlier, before the two circus performers had plunged to their separate deaths, before Rostnikov had failed to find his pickpocket, before the first faint light of dawn had tried to let the city know that it was waiting behind the clouds, a tall, gaunt man dressed in black had made his way to the records room of the Petrovka Station, had carefully collected notes in a black notebook, and had left the building to walk to the Marx Prospekt Metro Station, where he had climbed onto an arriving train and stood throughout his journey even though there were several seats available. Early-morning travelers avoided the man with the notebook. A pair of young women huddled together and whispered that the man looked like a vampire or, at best, a pale Tatar. Then, when he slowly turned toward them, they decided to change the subject completely. At the Komsomolskaya Station the man in black got off, his left arm stiffly at his side, the notebook clutched in his right hand. Through the window the two girls who were on their way to work looked out at the dark figure and decided that he was a murderer. As if hearing their words, the man turned his head and looked at them without expression. One of the girls let out a gasp as the train pulled away.

Emil Karpo had seen this reaction to him before, had heard criminals, policemen, whisper things about his frightening pallor or his almost religious zeal. He had heard the nicknames and he had not been bothered. In fact, he had felt that such nicknames helped to establish the relationship he wanted to have with the rest of the world. Rostnikov, whom Karpo admired with reservations, was known only as the Washtub, which somewhat accurately described the chief inspector's body but did not account for his strength or his puzzling attitude.

Karpo moved resolutely through the station without looking around at the decadent upturned glass chandeliers, the arched columns, and the curved white roof with decorative designs. He had seen the station thousands of times on his way from or to his small apartment and had long since decided that he preferred the more modern, efficient stations of the outer metro lines to this reminder of an earlier decadence. To Karpo, Russia meant sacrifice. The revolution was far from over, might never be over. There was only the struggle, the dedication, the small part one could play in the bigger picture. There wasn't necessarily a victory to be achieved. Life was a series of tests, challenges that one was either prepared for or would be worn away by. Since hardship was inevitable, it was best to condition oneself to it. Discomfort was welcome. Pain was the ultimate test. A weak individual could not function. There was a way in which one lived, as Lenin had lived. Emil Karpo was intelligent, unimaginative, determined, a zealous Marxist and an investigator in the Office of the Procurator General whom criminals feared with good reason.

Karpo walked slowly, deliberately clenching and unclenching his left fist as the surgeon who had operated on the arm had told him to do. The arm was, after three weeks, beginning to respond, and the doctor, a Jew named Alex who was related to Rostnikov's wife, had announced only the day before that Karpo would be using the arm and hand normally within four months. The entire incident had puzzled Karpo. The initial injury to the arm had been sustained after a fall from a ladder in pursuit of a minor confidence man. It had been reinjured in a terrorist explosion and dealt a further blow in a rooftop scuffle. Soviet doctors, three of them, had declared that Emil Karpo would never use his hand and arm again. He had resigned himself to this, considered his alternative values in Soviet society, and rejected Rostnikov's urging him to see Alex. But Alex had seen him, had promised results, had delivered. Karpo knew the system was not without its incompetents and fools. After all, that was why the police existed. But to have the medical system fail him so completely had given him some brooding hours.

A short walk later Karpo entered his apartment building. Though it was less than thirty years old, it smelled of mold and mildew and was not properly maintained. Karpo walked up the five flights of stairs. He would have done so even if there had been an elevator in the building, which there was not. As he always did, Karpo paused in the fifth-floor hallway, listened, waited, and then approached his door. Though he had no reason to expect intrusion, he checked the thin hair at the corner of the door just above the hinge to be sure no one had entered the room while he was out. Satisfied, Karpo inserted his key and stepped into the darkness.

It would have been dark in the room even if it were not a rainy morning, for Karpo always kept the black shade drawn. There was nothing out there he wanted to see. Out there was only another building across the courtyard. Windows, people, distractions.

Karpo moved to the center of the room in darkness and willed his left arm to reach up for the light cord. His arm told him that it was ridiculous, that the pain was not worth the satisfaction, but Karpo had dealt with the reluctance of his body before. In the darkness he clenched his teeth gently, held tightly to his notebook, and willed his left arm up. And up it went, feeling as if it had been dipped in hot metal. Slowly, up, up, and Karpo felt the cord on his fingers. He closed the fingers and demanded that his arm come down slowly, slowly, and it obeyed until the light came on, revealing the small room, nearly a cell, where Emil Karpo slept, worked, and occasionally ate. His brow was damp from his effort, but Karpo did not wipe it. He moved to the solid table desk in the corner, put down the black notebook, and turned on the desk lamp. Behind him was his bed, little more than a cot, neatly made. Next to the bed was a small table with a hot plate. Flat against one wall was a rough oak dresser. And that was it except for the bookshelves filled with black notebooks just like the one Karpo had placed on the desk. Each notebook was filled with reports, details on every case he had ever investigated or been part of. At night, when others slept, played, wept, drank, or laughed, Karpo went over his notebooks, studied the still-open cases.

It was Karpo's goal, though he knew he could never achieve it, to close every case in those black books, to catch and turn over for punishment every criminal. He reached up, took down a series of notebooks, placed them in a neat pile next to the one he had brought in, and removed a sheet of paper from the desk drawer, a sheet on which he had neatly ruled lines and filled in dates. It was not only his method, it was also his comfort. The room was a cool tomb where he could lose himself in his work, will himself to put everything in order. The books in front of him told Karpo that there was a killer on the streets of Moscow, a killer who had struck eight women in a little less than six years. The books told him that there was a pattern. Perhaps he did not have enough of the pattern yet to act, but a pattern was there, and tonight—or next month, or next year, or in ten years—he would find that pattern and find the killer.

He sat up straight, closed his eyes, concentrated on the moon he imagined, concentrated on nothing but the moon, watched it grow small as it moved away from him, and when it disappeared in the distance of his imagination, Karpo opened his eyes and went to work.

TWO

THE BABY WAS CRYING. SASHA TKACH ROLLED OVER and looked at the small crib next to his and Maya's bed. Then he groped on the nearby table for his watch. His right hand touched it and knocked it to the bare wooden floor, where it hit with a *thunk* barely heard over the baby's crying.

"What time?" Maya mumbled sleepily.

Sasha found the watch and tried to turn it so that he could read its face by the dim street light coming through the open window.

"I think it's two-twenty or maybe three-twenty," he said.

This revelation, or the sound of its parents' voices, made the baby cry a bit louder.

"She's hungry," said Maya, sitting up and rubbing her eyes.

"Hungry," agreed Sasha, flopping back on the bed.

He watched Maya rise, her full brown hair uncombed, the white American T-shirt she slept in clinging to her. Sasha smiled and closed his eyes. He could change Pulcharia's diaper, and was quite willing to do so, but he could not produce milk. Besides, Maya was on maternity leave and could sleep late if the baby let her.

In the weeks before the baby was born, Sasha's mother, Lydia, who slept in the next room, had loaded the pregnant Maya with old wives' tales and reasonable advice.

"Long walks, every day," Lydia had repeated, and Maya had agreed, walking to work in the early days of the pregnancy. "And no sweets. Sweets make the skin itch."

Maya had nodded with a tolerant smile at Sasha. Before the pregnancy, Maya had begun to show signs of irritation with her mother-in-law. Sasha well understood. During the day they were all at work—Lydia at the Ministry of Information, Sasha at Petrovka, and Maya at her most recent job, a day-care center for the workers at the Ts.U.M. department store on Petrov Street. But in the recent mornings and evenings, Lydia, who was growing increasingly deaf and increasingly irritable, made it difficult for the expectant parents to keep smiling. With only two rooms in the apartment, it was difficult to get away from each other, especially difficult to get away from Lydia's loud voice.

Sasha, eyes still closed, heard Maya pick up Pulcharia, coo to her. He opened his eyes and saw the dark silhouette of Maya, cross-legged on the floor, lifting her T-shirt to offer her full breast to the tiny girl named for Lydia's own mother, a concession Sasha thought was more than Maya should accept but to which Maya had readily agreed. She liked the old-fashioned name and really had no one in her family or in history or in literature that she particularly felt like naming her child for. Pulcharia seemed perfect to her.

Before the birth, Lydia had also announced, from her own experience and that of her few friends, that oxygen was essential to pregnant women. "So breathe deep when the contractions come and rub your stomach in circles like this. The pain will be like no other you have imagined."

"Thank you," Maya had said, smiling at Sasha.

When the baby did come, it was in the hospital, in a large delivery room from which Sasha was barred. Two other women were having babies at the same time. Maya had remembered the pain abstractly even when she told

Sasha about it. She remembered the white, loose gown they had put on her and tied at the neck. She remembered the screaming women on either side of her, the white-masked, white-gowned, white-capped quartet of doctors and nurses who helped her, and she remembered the pain. There was no anesthetic. Though the Lamaze method was developed largely through Soviet research, there was no encouragement to practice natural childbirth methods that might lessen pain. Pain was assumed to be a natural part of bearing a child. Pain, the doctor at the clinic had told her, was a reminder of the cost and responsibility of bearing a child. It was not supposed to be easy.

After the birth the baby had been kept from Maya for more than a full day to avoid infection. And though there was nothing wrong with mother or child, Sasha had been unable to see them for ten days. That, too, to avoid infection.

Sasha lay with his eyes closed, trying to remember the time he had seen on his watch. The watch was notoriously unreliable, a recent replacement for the pocket watch he had inherited from his father. The new watch was Romanian and tended to lose a minute every few days.

The baby was cooing now, and Maya was whispering, "*Krasee' v/iy doch*, beautiful daughter."

In another hour Sasha would have to get up, get dressed like a student, and hurry to a bookstall near Moscow State University that was reported to be a contact for the illegal sale of videotapes and videotape players. Sasha was a junior investigator in the Office of the Procurator General. He looked far younger than his twenty-nine years and was frequently used in undercover operations because of the innocence of his features. He looked nothing like a policeman. He also knew, and didn't like, the fact that among the investigators at Petrovka he had earned a nickname: the Innocent. Still, it was better to have a nickname, a reputation, a future, than to be where Rostnikov was now—demoted, for some reason, and under the eye of the Gray Wolfhound.

When next he opened his eyes, Sasha would get up

quietly, check on the baby, brush his teeth in the tiny bathroom that had no bath and a shower that infrequently worked, shave, dress, and grab a slice of bread and a drink of cool tea from the bottle in the small refrigerator. Then he would walk to the metro and head for the bookstall, where he would pretend to be a student wanting to buy a foreign videotape machine. His reports, which up to now had had little of substance in them, were not only being reviewed by Khabolov, the assistant procurator, but—because of the economic implications of the case, Sasha Tkach was sure—were also being examined by someone in the KGB. No one had told him this, but because the black market was involved it was obvious, and Khabolov's special interest in the case had made it clear that there was an urgency involved that was encountered only when pressure was being put on the assistant procurator.

Sasha felt Maya get back into the bed, cover herself with the thin sheet, and move close to him. The baby was quiet. Somewhere far away through the open window a drunken voice laughed once and then was silent. Sasha reached over and put his arm around his wife. She moved his hand to her belly and for a moment there was a soft silence. But only for a moment. The door to Lydia's small bedroom shot open and Sasha's mother's voice squealed out in exasperation.

"Can't the two of you hear the baby crying?"

With that, of course, Pulcharia woke up again and began to cry.

"Details, routine, vigilance," the Gray Wolfhound announced, holding up one finger of his slender hand to emphasize each word.

Two men sitting at the table in the meeting room at the Petrovka Station looked up at Colonel Snitkonoy and nodded in agreement. The third man, Porfiry Petrovich Rostnikov, was barely aware of the words at all. He was aware of the standing colonel, the tall, slender man with the distinguished gray temples whose brown uniform was perfectly pressed, whose three ribbons of honor, neatly aligned on his chest, were just right in both color and number. The colonel was impressive. And that, indeed, was his primary function: to impress visitors and underlings; to stride, hands clasped behind his back like a czarist general deep in thought about an impending battle. So successful was the Gray Wolfhound at his role that it was rumored that a Bulgarian journalist had returned to Sofia and written a novel with Snitkonoy as the very evident model for his heroic policeman hero.

"Your thoughts, Comrades," Snitkonoy said, waving his hand before again clasping it behind his back. He was the only one standing, poised in front of a blackboard on which he had occasionally been known to make lists and to write words that he wanted those with whom he met to remember.

Two of the men at the table looked at each other to determine which of them might have a thought. They ignored Rostnikov, who doodled on the pad in front of him.

One of the men at the table was the Gray Wolfhound's assistant, Pankov, a near-dwarf of a man with thinning hair who was widely believed to hold his job because he made such a perfect contrast to the colonel. Pankov was a perspirer, always uncertain. His clothes were perpetually rumpled, his few strands of hair unwilling to lie in peace against his scalp. When he stood, Pankov came up to the Wolfhound's chest. In appreciation of Pankov's flattering inadequacy, the colonel never failed to treat his assistant with patronizing respect.

Opposite Pankov sat the uniformed Major Grigorovich, a solid, ambitious block of a man in his early forties who saw himself as the eventual heir to the Wolfhound and took pride in his ability to keep Snitkonoy from feeling threatened while making clear to his colleagues that he, Major Andrei Grigorovich, was no fool. On his second day with the Wolfhound, Rostnikov had commented to his wife, Sarah, that Grigorovich looked a bit like a slightly overweight version of the British actor Albert Finney. Occasionally during these briefing sessions, Rostnikov would draw little caricatures of Grigorovich, Pankov, Snitkonoy, or one of the others who sometimes joined them to give reports.

It was believed among all who attended the sessions that the Washtub, Rostnikov, was taking detailed notes on everything everyone said. Rostnikov's reputation as a criminal investigator added an air of intimidation to the morning meetings, and much speculation existed over why he had been assigned to basic criminal investigation. Pankov, who shared his views with everyone who would listen, was convinced that Rostnikov was there to evaluate the Gray Wolfhound. Pankov knew that if the Wolfhound fell, so would he. Therefore, Pankov was ever alert to undermine suggestions Rostnikov might make, while at the same time trying to keep Rostnikov from knowing what he was doing because Rostnikov might well later hurt those who had given him trouble. This difficult position resulted in Pankov's seldom speaking at the meetings for fear of offending anyone. Grigorovich was convinced that Rostnikov was being considered to replace the Wolfhound, or at least to be tested against Grigorovich to determine which man should, either soon or in the distant future, move up a notch.

Snitkonoy, on the other hand, simply assumed that Rostnikov had been assigned to him so that he, Rostnikov, could learn the nuances of leadership that he lacked so he could return to the Procurator's Office at some point in the future with a new sense of purpose and the inspiration provided by his association with Snitkonoy.

And that was the situation that prevailed in the room when the three men at the table were asked for their thoughts. It was evident to all of them that their real thoughts were the last things they would give in this room. It was also evident to Rostnikov that none of them had really been paying attention to the Wolfhound.

"We must continue to tighten up on our efficiency," Pankov said, taking the easy, abstract route and pounding his small fist into his palm for emphasis.

"Yes," said the Gray Wolfhound with tolerance but no enthusiasm. "Major?"

"We must have an adequate termination of a greater per-

centage of our cases, our responsibilities," said Grigorovich, looking at Rostnikov, who continued to frown at the
pad of paper on which he was doodling.

"Paperwork, evidence, must be more complete, investigations better documented, before we turn each case over
to the Procurator's Office for prosecution or further investigation," Grigorovich went on.

"Yes," Pankov agreed.

"Comrade Inspector," the Wolfhound said, snapping the
pointing finger of his right hand at Rostnikov. "Your
views? You have had time to gather your thoughts. Perhaps
your delay this morning was due to your diligence in pre-
paring for this meeting?"

"This morning," said Rostnikov slowly, his eyes coming
up from the poor copy of Gogol's statue he was working
on, "a man leaped to his death from the new Gogol statue."

The silence was long as they waited for Rostnikov to
continue. Outside and below them, in the police-dog com-
pound, a German shepherd began to bark and then suddenly went quiet. When it became evident that Rostnikov
had no thoughts of continuing, Snitkonoy prodded as he
stepped back and tilted his head.

"And the point of this, Comrade Inspector?"

Grigorovich and Pankov turned their eyes to Rostnikov,
who sighed, shrugged, and looked up.

"I wondered what would so frighten a man that he
would do a thing like that," Rostnikov mused. "Leap headfirst to the pavement. Crush his skull like an overripe to-
mato."

"Was there some evidence of intimidation, some suggestion of murder?" Pankov asked, wondering if this were
some kind of test by Rostnikov.

"It's not important," Rostnikov said, pushing the pad
away. "Might I suggest that we proceed to the case list and
make the assignments?"

The Wolfhound was puzzled, but the Wolfhound was
better than a professional actor. His eyes fixed knowingly,
sympathetically, on Rostnikov, as if he knew exactly what
was on the inspector's mind. Then he turned his eyes to the

neat black vinyl folder in front of him. The colonel opened the file, now anxious to go through the routine and get the brooding Rostnikov out of the room. He had hoped for a concluding half hour or more of philosophical musing and teaching, but Rostnikov had poisoned the atmosphere.

Snitkonoy flipped open the folder and scanned the list of new cases for the morning. All had already been assigned to the investigators who took the initial calls, except for three that had been appropriated by the KGB. Those cases had thick black lines through them, lines so thick and so black that one could make out no trace of a single letter designating the case. The Wolfhound's gray eyes scanned the list and then he grinned—a private, knowing grin—as he passed out copies of the new case list to the three men in the room.

"Comrades, do you see anything of special concern on this list? Any cases you would like transferred to other investigators? Concentrated upon?"

It was the routine morning speech, but the list was not routine for Rostnikov, who had expected simply to be assigned to an additional case or two without great consequence or meaning. And then his eye caught the description of Case Number 16. He let his head come up lazily, hiding his reaction. A show of enthusiasm or real interest might doom his chances. The very fact that he wanted the case might be reason enough for the Wolfhound to demonstrate his power and assign it to someone else.

"Number five," Grigorovich said. "The increased activity of assaults on old people near the war memorial suggests . . ."

It went on like that for twenty minutes. Rostnikov made a point about reexamination of the evidence from a family murder the week before. He supported Grigorovich's interest in the assault case and, though he thought it was idiotic, nodded in agreement when Pankov suggested a consolidation of four cases, all of which dealt with reports of illegal sales of vodka. There was clearly no relationship among the cases other than the recent interest in alcoholism that

Gorbachev had been pushing for the past year. It was fashionable to denounce alcoholism.

Now that Grigorovich and Pankov each owed him something, Rostnikov made his move.

"Number thirty-four," he said. "The report of several assaults in parks. It may be a pattern. Other than that, nothing seems to need further attention, though there are a few cases that might be worth a minor review of initial investigation. Numbers"—he scanned the list casually—"three, twelve, sixteen, and twenty-four."

The other three men scanned the list and nodded, not seeing anything worth checking in any of the cases, but not wanting it to seem as if they had missed something.

"Fine," sighed the Wolfhound, closing his vinyl file, placing it on the table, and slapping his palm against it. "If you have time, Comrade Inspector, you can review initial investigations on those cases. Number thirty-four, the assaults, I think should be supervised by Sergei Pankov."

Pankov smiled in triumph, and Rostnikov and Grigorovich nodded in agreement.

"Good," said the Wolfhound. "I have a report to give at the People's Court in Podolski this afternoon. Since we got started a bit late"—and with this he paused for less than a breath to let his eyes fall on Rostnikov before he continued —"there will be no time for progress reports on continuing investigations. We will, therefore, meet tomorrow morning at six for progress reports. Inspector Rostnikov, this note is for you."

The Wolfhound produced an envelope from behind his back and handed it to Rostnikov. Without waiting for comment, the Wolfhound turned and strode out of the room, his shiny black boots clapping against the tile floor.

Grigorovich and Pankov placed their various papers into folders, tucked the folders under their arms, and uttered a clipped "Good morning, Comrades" as they exited.

Alone, Rostnikov looked up at the single window for the first time since he had entered the room. His leg had grown stiff, his clothes were still wet, and he knew it was still raining. The envelope the colonel had handed him was grayish-white, unmarked. Nothing was written on it. Rostnikov slit the top flap with his fingernail. The note was brief, typed. He looked out at the rain, sighed, and stood up. He would have to take the metro, but he should still make it by the time indicated in the letter.

Before he left the building, he went to the central desk and said that he wanted a copy of the report on Case Number 16 for that morning.

"Case Number?" the short-haired woman behind the desk asked, looking at the stack of files in front of her.

"Oleg Pesknoko, the circus performer who died this morning," Rostnikov said.

"Ah," said the woman triumphantly, locating the file and handing it to Rostnikov. "The accident."

"Yes," Rostnikov said, tucking the file under his arm. "The accident."

The man who had killed eight prostitutes in the past six years had no idea on that Monday morning that Investigator Emil Karpo of the Procurator's Office was looking for him. Yuri Pon really didn't worry about the police at all, because he was well aware of the official status of the investigation of his activities. He was aware of the progress, or lack of it, because he worked in the central records department of the Office of the Procurator General of Moscow.

Pon had not even checked the files for the possibility of any recent activity. No one really cared about the prostitutes. There were too many other priorities: murders, maimings, crimes against the state. Since prostitutes did not officially exist any longer, the file referred to the victims as "women of questionable character." Pon referred to them, and only to himself and his diary, as the snakes.

Since he was a boy, Pon, who was nearing his forty-first birthday, had seen these women and had sensed, knew, what they were. He had seen them, been fascinated by the prostitutes who hung around the railway stations and the others who sat in hotel lobbies or restaurants on Gorky Street. He had seen them, dreamed of them, even wanted them, though he was repulsed by the idea. There was no possibility that Yuri Pon would actually go to bed with a prostitute.

As he sat at his desk, stamping the folders in front of him with an official seal, he shook his head to confirm his determination. He would never go with a prostitute. It would be like . . . like wrapping a snake around your most private parts, the way he had wrapped a cloth in the tub when he was a child. But it would be more smooth and scaly. Yuri Pon shuddered. The shudder ran through his puttylike body. Nausea made him lift his eyes and peer through his glasses toward the washroom. But the feeling passed and he sat back, furiously stamping, stamping, stamping.

And why had this come on? He had been drinking the night before. That was true. But that wasn't unusual. Had he been drinking the night before it had happened the other times? He didn't remember. Perhaps he had, but there had also been many nights when he had consumed far more vodka, felt far more the pull and repulsion of the prostitutes, especially the one at the restaurant on Gorky.

"Comrade Pon," a voice broke in.

Pon shook and almost dropped the seal in his hand.

"Pon," the woman repeated.

"Yes," Pon answered, adjusting his glasses and looking up at Ludmilla Kropetskanoya, the assistant files supervisor, who always wore black and looked like a light pole.

"File these." She handed him a half dozen files and strode away from his desk toward the stairs. "And try to hurry with this busywork and get back to the computer."

Pon watched her leave, feeling nothing but a vague dizziness from the drinking of the night before. As he rose he continued to wonder why he was thinking about the prostitutes once more. Was he going to start having those nights again? The nights when the feeling wouldn't go away? Night after night after night, feeling his body in the darkness, responding to the memories of those women, responding but never satisfied. The killings had given him relief, great relief. But the feeling had always come back.

Pon tucked the sheets of new information and reports under his left arm and pushed the odd pieces of paper back into the files as he walked slowly to the rows of drawers behind him. He paused at the white plastic table, stacked the files, and began to sort them by case number.

It had been almost a full year since he had last needed to find a prostitute. Though he was too cautious to be certain, still he hoped that it might mean that the feeling was gone for good. He liked his job, liked the two-room apartment he shared with Nikolai. He enjoyed filing. It took little thought and gave him a feeling of accomplishment and plenty of time to think. These were his files—neat, not a report sticking up, not a file frayed—and soon, within months perhaps, he and the others would have everything fully transferred to the computers. Though he had a limited supply of new file—

It was with this thought that Pon froze and stared at the file in his hand. Number 1265-0987. It was the only file number in the whole system he had memorized, because he felt it was his, the file detailing all of his dispositions of prostitutes. He had kept it even more orderly than the rest. He wanted it to remain untouched, perfect, safe.

And now, almost a year after anyone had looked at it, someone had come, probably during the overnight shift, and pulled the file. Yuri had mixed feelings. Fear and excitement made his hands tremble, and he had a shiver of something almost mystical. He had thought little about that file, about those feelings, about what he had had to do, for months. But this morning he had come in sensing, feeling, the echo of it all again. The reason was clear.

He had somehow known that someone was thinking about him. It was uncanny and frustrating, for there was no one he could tell about this.

Nikolai had once said that when he had the pains in his side he had awakened during the night and had seen a huge, clear letter C embossed on his skin at the point of the greatest pain. The C had been formed by a pebbly ridge of flesh. "I was sure, I knew, that in spite of the impossibility," Nikolai had said, leaning forward as if he were telling a great secret, "my body was informing me that I had cancer. Only it was stranger than that. I did not have cancer, only dyspepsia. I had told myself "—and with this Nikolai pointed a dark finger at his head—"that I had cancer. My mind had been strong enough to generate a change in my skin. Amazing."

Perhaps, somehow, this was what had happened to Yuri Pon this morning, but he could never tell Nikolai or his mother or anyone. Then a horrible half image came to him, a half image of himself telling not only of this uncanny incident but of everything he thought and felt, telling all this to a gaunt man who looked like a dark priest.

Yuri blinked his eyes, put down the files, and adjusted his glasses before he felt strong enough to open his file. The name of the person who had checked it out this very morning was written in a tall, firm hand that kept the letters neat and within the lines: Emil Karpo. Yuri Pon knew the name. Karpo had checked the file out sixteen times in the past eight years, far more than any other investigator, though Karpo was not even the principal investigator on the case.

Perhaps, thought Yuri the file clerk, Yuri the killer of prostitutes, there is some new piece of evidence, but what could there be that was new? What could Karpo know?

Yuri knew who Karpo was, had seen him frequently, had seen his name on hundreds of files. Karpo the Vampire, that was what he had heard an investigator named Zelach call him. Yuri Pon tried not to think about the image of a vampire. He tried to force himself to review everything that was in the file. He had done it a thousand times and never had he been able to follow any trail that would lead to him. He had been too careful. Knowing how the investigators worked, he had avoided mistakes, controlled his emotions each time. He was proud of that, proud of that control.

Coincidence, just a coincidence. Karpo was reviewing files, randomly reviewing files. Yuri would check, see what other files the Vam—, no, what other files Inspector Karpo had recently pulled out. There was nothing to worry about, nothing. Yuri put his file and the others away and spent the next two hours before lunch neatly typing new file numbers into the computer for the cases that would come in. Thought almost disappeared as he typed, and when his watch told him that he could stop and eat he smiled. It was under control. And then as he sat at his desk and lifted the small round bread from the sack in the drawer, a horrible thought sickened him.

What, he thought, if Karpo knows? What if he knows and is playing a game with me? What if he was watching when the file was returned, is watching right now? Yuri turned quickly from this corner to that, down the row of files, toward the stairway leading up to the next level, to the ceiling where, perhaps, someone had planted a camera.

Yuri Pon couldn't swallow. He was afraid he would choke. He clutched for the bottle of kvass in his sack, unscrewed it, and drank deeply, almost choking.

Madness, he thought. No one is watching me. No one. But that was not the problem. A new one had come. He was sure now. Absolutely sure that the feeling was back, that this very night it would begin again, that the memory of the prostitute in the restaurant would be with him, driving him mad until he dealt with it. Karpo couldn't be watching him. No, but Yuri Pon would certainly be watching Emil Karpo. He finished the small bottle of kvass, let out a small burp, and wondered how he would get through the rest of the day.

The rain had almost stopped when Rostnikov arrived and stood across the street in front of the building to which he had been ordered. The four-story building had no sign on its door to mark its function or purpose. It looked like a small factory, perhaps a complex of offices. There were eleven windows on the street side, each covered so that no one could see in. The concrete facade was smooth, gray, and very common. If one stood across the street where Rostnikov then stood one could see on the roof of the third floor a patio and a series of canopies that looked as if they belonged at the beach in Yalta.

Officially, this building had no name. It didn't exist. Unofficially, and to almost every Muscovite who passed it, it was the Kremlin Polyclinic, where the nation's "special" people went for medical care. Rostnikov crossed the street slowly, glanced at a man with a thick shiny leather brief-case who was reading the copy of *Pravda* posted on the corner bulletin board, and walked past the single car parked at the curb. It was a long, black four-door Zil, a monster of a car that needed only teeth. Only members of the Politburo were issued Zils. It was estimated that no more than fifteen of the custom automobiles were made each year.

Rostnikov glanced at the car and at the man behind the wheel in the front seat, a young man in a dark suit and a firmly knotted tie, a young man who looked as if his nose had been smashed with a hammer. The young man glanced at Rostnikov and then looked resolutely out the car's front window.

Rostnikov entered the building and found himself facing a pair of burly men in identical blue suits. Both men were in their forties and had close-cropped hair. Beyond them in the small lobby was a desk at which a man and a woman sat. The man was talking quietly on the phone. The woman was looking over her glasses and appeared to be copying something. Only their heads were visible over the level of the desk. Rostnikov imagined for an instant that both of them had been beheaded and were on display at the Poly-clinic to prove how capable and experimental the staff was. Perhaps, he thought, the two heads will even sing a folk song in unison. The image brought a small smile to Rost-nikov's face, which, in turn, brought a look of suspicion to the face of the slightly older of the two burly men, who stepped in Rostnikov's path.

"You have business here, Comrade?" the burly man asked.

Rostnikov gauged the two. Certainly KGB. Both were younger, bigger, more agile than Rostnikov, and both, as evidenced by their slightly bulky jackets, had weapons— hidden but handy. Still, Rostnikov was sure that if they attempted to throw him out, he would probably have little trouble getting past them. It was only whimsy, however, for Porfiry Petrovich had no real urge to force his way past the KGB. He didn't even want to be here. Rostnikov reached into his pocket and handed the older of the two men the note Snitkonoy had given him less than an hour earlier. The KGB man ran his right palm over the top of his bristly hair before taking the offering. Rostnikov and the second man looked at each other silently while the first man read the note quickly.

"This way," the reader said, handing the note back to Rostnikov and turning toward the desk. Rostnikov followed him slowly, sandwiched between him and the other burly man. Rostnikov had followed the KGB before. His leg didn't permit him to keep up the pace of these younger men eager to show that everything was urgent. Rostnikov was in no hurry. He had nowhere he wanted to go other than the circus and home. So he walked slowly past the desk where the decapitated head of the woman whose hair was tied back in a bun looked up at him over her glasses.

The parade of three went through a darkly stained wooden door and into an elevator that stood open. They entered silently and faced front, and the younger man pressed a button that closed the doors. He then pressed a button for the third floor and they rode up smoothly. At three, the elevator stopped with a small bounce, the doors opened, and the older KGB officer stepped out. Rostnikov followed, with the younger man behind him.

To the right was a corridor with closed doors. At the far end of the corridor was a desk behind which stood a pair of men clad in white. Talking, they paid no attention to the three men who moved about twenty feet down the corridor and went through a door.

Rostnikov found himself on an outdoor, wooden-floored patio. There were a series of chairs and a scattering of white metal tables on the long patio, as if someone had thrown a party and neglected to take the last step of putting back the furniture.

In one of the chairs, under a canopy, sat a very old man

in a dark robe. He was the only one on the patio, and he seemed to be asleep, his eyes closed, as the three men approached.

"Comrade," the older KGB man said softly as they stood in front of the dozing old man. The old man didn't answer.

"Comrade," the older KGB man repeated, perhaps a little uncertain if he should pursue this or simply wait.

"Yes," said the old man, his eyes still closed.

"The man you sent for has arrived," said the KGB man, looking at his partner for some kind of support.

The old man opened his eyes, blinked at the sun, ran his heavily veined hands through his crop of billowy white hair, and sat up. He was small, his face deeply lined, with little broken blood vessels under the eyes that might indicate vodka or age, or both. He didn't look up, but groped in the pocket of his robe for his glasses, found them, placed them on his nose, and looked at the polished wooden floor, shaking his head once. Only then did he look up at Rostnikov. Rostnikov met his eyes and showed nothing.

"You two," the old man said. "Get back downstairs."

The KGB men nodded, turned, and departed.

When they had left, the old man, still sitting, bit his thin lower lip gently and watched Rostnikov, who stood solidly, resisting the urge to rock.

"You may sit, Inspector," said the old man.

"Thank you, Colonel," Rostnikov answered and made his way to a chair, turning it to face the old man. They were perhaps ten feet apart and Rostnikov felt decidedly uneasy. Rostnikov had dealt with this old man before, had sparred with him, tried to trick him, had blackmailed him, and had earned his enmity. That Colonel Drozhkin had offered him a seat was a very bad sign. Drozhkin normally preferred to have Rostnikov stand on the leg the colonel knew would ache painfully after four or five minutes.

"You are getting along in your new duties, Inspector?" Drozhkin asked, this time looking away to show that the question was not a sincere or meaningful one, that Rostnikov would have to play, appear uncurious, till Drozhkin was willing to get to the point, a point he would probably not come to directly.

"I am doing my best," Rostnikov said.

"But," said Drozhkin with a falsely sympathetic smile, "it is a bit less . . . responsible than your former duties, and Colonel Snitkonoy has methods that are"—he held up his withered hands in a gesture of resignation—"you know what I mean."

"I believe I do, Comrade Colonel," said Rostnikov. "But I find Colonel Snitkonoy an inspiration, and my duties, no matter how inconsequential they appear, to be a meaningful part of the state's efforts to bring an end to all criminal activity."

The old man shrugged his shoulders as if a cold wind had cut through him.

"Not many months ago your desire to aid in preserving the ideals of our nation were less compelling than your desire to seek your fortune in a Western country, a decadent country," said Drozhkin. "Would you like some tea?"

"No, thank you, Comrade," Rostnikov said. "I am convinced that my interest in departing was a brief incapacitation brought on by a heavy work schedule."

The two men sat silently for a moment, having restated the stalemate they had lived under for almost a year. Rostnikov had thought he had sufficient evidence of a KGB conspiracy to murder dissidents, a conspiracy that would have embarrassed the government at a time when the official policy was one of overt reconciliation, of placating the non-Soviet-aligned nations. Rostnikov had managed to get his evidence out of the country with a German tourist. He had approached Drozhkin with the suggestion that he, Rostnikov, his Jewish wife, Sarah, and their son, Josef, be allowed to emigrate under the Jewish quota.

Rostnikov had underestimated the KGB's resolve and possibly the value of his own information, especially after two premiers had died and the possibility existed that Gorbachev could simply accept the truth of the charges and blame them on Andropov or even Brezhnev. The result had been a stalemate. Rostnikov could live. His wife could work. His son could remain in the army without fear of "special" treatment. And Rostnikov could go on working under close supervision. It was the best that either side could do, and Rostnikov was confident that the KGB had agents in Western Europe trying to find the evidence he had smuggled out. If they ever found it . . .

"Life is complicated," Drozhkin said, as if reading Rostnikov's thoughts.

"Yes," agreed Rostnikov. "We must learn to accept and live with complication."

"Live with it carefully," Drozhkin corrected.

"Very carefully," Rostnikov said.

Drozhkin smiled, but it was a smile Rostnikov didn't like.

"I'm dying," Drozhkin said, his dark eyes fixed on Rostnikov's face. Rostnikov had been expecting something and showed no reaction. He was certain that this was not the news Drozhkin had brought him to hear. He and the KGB colonel were far from friends. This was a distraction to set him up, weaken him, throw him off balance before he learned the real reason for the summoning. However, Rostnikov had no doubt that the colonel's announcement of his coming death was true.

"I'm sorry to hear this, Comrade," Rostnikov said flatly.

"You should be," said the old man. "My protective interest in you will be turned over to my assistant, Major Zhenya. You remember Major Zhenya?"

"I remember Major Zhenya," Rostnikov acknowledged.

Zhenya was not one to forget. Rostnikov called up the image of the tall, lean, straight-backed man who had led him to Drozhkin's office the few times Rostnikov had been summoned to Lubyanka. Zhenya had taken pleasure in staying far enough in front of Rostnikov to make the inspector limp in embarrassment after him. Only Rostnikov had not hurried to keep up with him the second time this happened. Rostnikov had instead slowed down, knowing that Zhenya would not risk failing to deliver the visitor to the quite crotchety old colonel. Zhenya did not like Rostnikov. There may have been a reason, but Rostnikov had no idea what it might be. It was not peculiar to the KGB to take a sudden and lifelong dislike to someone. It was common in the Soviet Union. It was, however, particularly dangerous to have a KGB man dislike you. The dying old colonel's face remained placid, but Rostnikov was sure he had enjoyed passing on the information about Zhenya.

They sat quietly for a moment or two, and then the door beyond the canopy behind Rostnikov opened and a young man with rimless glasses stepped out. He was wearing white and carrying a tray on which rested a steaming pot and two white cups. The man put the tray down on the table and poured a cup of tea.

"Perhaps the sun and air have changed your mind?" asked Drozhkin.

"Perhaps," said Rostnikov. "A cup of tea would be refreshing."

The young man poured a second cup of tea and handed it to the inspector. The two men sat in silence under the sun and sipped tea till the young man in white left.

"Would you like to know what I am dying of?" Drozhkin said, making a slightly sour face and putting down his tea.

Rostnikov didn't answer. He sipped his tea.

"I am dying of many things, impending mandatory retirement is the most vivid to me, but to the doctors it is a cancer that has decided to inhabit the organs of my body. If a cancer could be given intellect, one might reason with it, suggest to it that it live a careful, parasitic existence so it would not destroy its host, but cancers are self-destructive. I am almost seventy-four, not a very old man, but not a young one. I am not well educated, Porfiry Petrovich Rostnikov, but I have managed to survive many changes in leadership, to retain my rank, and barring a disaster, to die with dignity for myself and my family."

The point, Rostnikov was sure, was now being approached.

"You have had a long and distinguished career, Comrade Colonel, and I'm sure you have been an inspiration to your friends and family."

"Your son has been posted to Afghanistan," Drozhkin said, sipping the tea again and finding it no more acceptable.

This was it. Rostnikov wanted to get up, take the five paces across the roof, and hurl the withered old man over the edge of the roof to the street below. Instead he picked up the tea, willed his thick hands to be steady, and sipped. The tea was no longer hot, but he drank it all, knowing that Drozhkin's eyes were on him.

"The decision was not mine," Drozhkin said. "I suggested that he remain in Kiev, within the Soviet Union, but there are others above me. And considering recent events in Kiev, it may be that Afghanistan is not the worst place he could be."

Still Rostnikov said nothing. Josef was his and Sarah's only son. This threat had hung over them since Rostnikov had first run afoul of the KGB. Posting his son to the dangers of Afghanistan was a challenge, a test on which not only Josef's but also his and Sarah's lives were at stake. Rostnikov had one other piece of information about a KGB department head, a piece of information he knew he could never use. He also knew that he was now being tested to see if he were foolish enough to even hint that he might make use of such a secret. The KGB, through this dying old man, had raised the stakes, used Josef as the pawn, and Rostnikov had no choice but to back down.

"If my son is needed in Afghanistan, or any other place where the Soviet Union might be called, I am sure he will be honored to be chosen, as my wife and I will be honored to have him serve."

It was Drozhkin's turn to say nothing. He watched Rostnikov drink his tea, met his eyes. He saw neither fear nor hatred in the eyes of the burly inspector before him, but Drozhkin had survived by distrusting the evidence of his own eyes.

"That is all," Drozhkin said. "I must rest now."

Rostnikov put down his cup carefully, resisting the urge

to drop it and apologize. He stood up quite slowly.

"I hope you feel better, Comrade," he said to the old man, "and that the doctors make your final days as comfortable as you deserve."

There was no derision in Rostnikov's tone, nothing but apparent concern. Drozhkin knew better and approved. Some small token of rebellion or anger was necessary. Drozhkin would not accept complete capitulation by Rostnikov. Rostnikov, however, understood the same thing and had quickly calculated the level of affront and the delivery essential to create the proper impression. They were both experts at the game.

"This hospital has all the best," Drozhkin said, nodding over his shoulder. "There's not a piece of equipment in here manufactured in the Soviet Union, not one piece. American, Japanese, Swedish. Even the doctors are imported. Romanians, Poles, even a Frenchman. I get the best of attention here, which means I'll live a few days longer than I would have and I'll not die in agony. I accept what must be."

"As do I," said Rostnikov with a slight bow of his head.

When Rostnikov hit the lobby of the hospital he did not look at the two KGB men. He did not look at the two heads on the desk. He did not look at the old woman being led through the door by two men in white. Rostnikov put down his head and limped across the floor and out the front door. On the street he breathed deeply and looked around. Nothing had changed. Of course not, nothing but his life. He would have to go home later, have to tell Sarah, have to live in fear for his son, have to do his job, have to control his frustration, his anger. And then he remembered the circus, the Old Moscow Circus. His father had taken him to the Old Circus on Tvetnoi Boulevard when he was a boy. He remembered the lights outside, the two prancing horses above the entrance, the smell of animals. Then he remembered taking Josef to the New Circus on Vernadsky Prospekt, the new round building of steel and glass topped with multicolored pennants waving through a shower of searchlights. And inside . . . Yes, he decided, it was definitely time to get to the circus.

Sasha Tkach got off the train at the Universitet Metro Station almost an hour to the minute before Rostnikov would come to the same station. Rostnikov would walk one block down Vernadsky Prospekt in the direction of the Moscow River and find himself in front of the New Circus. Sasha, however, went up the escalator, left the station, and moved down Lomonosov Prospekt in the direction of the new building of Moscow State University. This massive building, completed in 1953, with its tall, thirty-two-story central spire, looked like a cathedral, standing high above any other building in the Lenin Hills area. Atop the spire was a golden star set in ears of wheat. On the flanking eighteen- and twelve-story buildings alongside the central structure were a giant clock, a thermometer, and a barometer that students, faculty, workers, and visitors could glance up at as they moved down the long pathway, the Walk of Fame, to the central building, a pathway decorated with inspirational busts of Russian scientists and scholars.

The university covered forty blocks with research facilities. There were botanical gardens, a sports stadium, and a huge park. There was a fine arts assembly hall that could seat 1,500, a student club, 19 lecture theaters, 140 auditoriums, dozens of teaching and research laboratories, the Museum of Earth Sciences, a swimming pool, sports facilities, and 6,000 rooms for students.

To be a student at Moscow State University, Tkach knew as he hurried in the direction of the spire, was to be admitted to the elite. The trick was to do well enough to make it to the university, to pass the tests, to have the connections in the Party, to say the right things, be in the right places. The attrition rate of students entering the university was very small. The reasons were both simple and not so simple. First, the students who got in were selected carefully, though politically. They were good, well suited for the education they would receive. Second, the future of the faculty was dependent on how well students performed.

Students were protected once they entered to insure that they would succeed and reflect well on their departments, their teachers, the university. Students at Moscow State University and the other major Soviet universities were well treated and had comfortable rooms, good food, and access to cultural and leisure opportunities that were paralleled only by the politically elite in the Communist Party.

Sasha Tkach knew all this as he hurried down the street, clutching a briefcase filled not with lecture notes and textbooks but with his lunch and a war novel. He saw real students pass him, felt resentment and fear that someone, perhaps the dark, short-haired girl then in front of him, would stop and say, "That is no student. That is a fraud, an undereducated fraud."

On Lomonosov Prospekt, behind the university, he saw the bookstall. It looked ordinary enough, a large table in front of a fairly large white trailer in need of a painting. Sasha shifted his briefcase from his sweating right hand to his left, pushed his hair out of his eyes, and made his way through the small crowd to the table. Information on the bookstall as a possible outlet for black market video equipment had come from a small-scale dealer in black market records, Tsimion Gaidar, who claimed to have traded a supply of Beatles records for a videotape machine through the bookstall. Gaidar's information was suspect, since he was trying to save himself from black market charges and the KGB. In addition, Gaidar had been known in the past to try to turn in anyone in his acquaintance, including his own brother, to escape prosecution.

However, Deputy Procurator Khabolov had decided that Sasha's mission was worth a try.

Sasha gently elbowed his way next to a man in a blue hooded sweatshirt. The man was wearing a cap and looked like a cab driver, but he could have been a professor or just a maintenance worker at the university. The rest of the crowd was a bit easier for Sasha to place—students, smiling more than most Muscovites, smiling as if they had a secret for success.

Tkach asked the small woman behind the table if she

had anything for children. The woman, a dumpy, dour creature wearing a dark dress too warm for the weather, nodded, meaning that he should go farther down the table, and Sasha muscled and apologized his way along to follow her. The books were all covered by glass to prevent theft. Each customer had to ask to examine any of the books, guides, or maps, and the woman kept a careful eye on all to whom she granted the right to touch the precious pages.

"That one," Sasha said, pointing at a thin book of Lermontov fairy tales with a colorful cover. The dour woman nodded, gently pulled the book from under the glass, and handed it to Sasha. A customer farther along the table called to the woman, who paused to examine Sasha, decided to take a chance on leaving the book with him, and shuffled over to the caller.

Tkach, clutching his briefcase, flipped through the pages but looked over them at the trailer. A pretty but unsmiling little girl of about eight years stood next to the trailer. She was dressed for school, her dress short for the summer, her dark hair tied with two yellow bows. She stood on one leg, swinging her other leg back and forth. She was looking at Sasha and the book. He held it up toward her. The girl glanced at the woman dealing with another customer and quickly shook her head no at Sasha, who nodded. Sasha pointed down at a series of books under the glass. To each one the girl shook her head no while checking to be sure the woman did not see her. As he pointed to the fifth book, the girl gave a small but emphatic nod of yes.

When the woman moved back down to Sasha, he handed her the book of fairy tales and pointed at the book the little girl had approved. The dour woman quickly turned her head toward the little girl, but the child was looking beyond the scene toward the Lenin Hills.

"I'll take it," he said. "*Sko' l' ka sto' eet*? How much?"

"One ruble," the woman said.

Sasha had not intended to buy anything, knew he would not be reimbursed by the Procurator's Office. He did have an advance for enough money to purchase a record album as evidence. There was a procedure for reimbursement, but it was complicated and required anticipation of one's expenditures, the filling out of a form, and long waits. The woman took the book and wrapped it, and Sasha felt a sudden feeling of pleasure. His smile was sincere. He had purchased his first book for his daughter, for Pulcharia. He was about to tell the woman when he thought better of it. He was a student. What was a young student doing with a baby daughter? He wasn't sure how common such a thing was. So instead of a thank you or an explanation, when he reached over to take the book he said softly to the woman, "Do you carry records?"

The woman looked at him as he took the book and shook her head in a decided no, but she did not hide the touch of caution in the corner of her large mouth. As she started to turn away, Tkach added conversationally, "A man from whom I purchased a record said you might have one I wanted. And I want it very badly."

The woman ignored him, or appeared to, and began to wait on a young woman with long blond hair and glasses. The young woman, who carried several books, glanced at Sasha and smiled, which marked her immediately as a student even if her youth and the books had not. He looked back at her but didn't smile.

"The man who recommended you is named Gaidar, Tsimion Gaidar," Sasha went on. "I've purchased several recordings from him."

The dour woman behind the table moved over to him quickly, ignoring a man with a gray beard who called to her impatiently and looked at his watch. The dour woman looked at Sasha's open, boyish face, and he did his best to look open, innocent, the Innocent.

"Behind the trailer," the woman said, leaning forward. "Knock at the door."

With this she backed away. Sasha glanced at the little girl at the trailer and held up his wrapped book. She nodded in approval, and Sasha backed through the dozen or so people at the table, opened his briefcase, and put the book inside. He hadn't even checked to see what the book was.

The back of the white trailer looked much like the front. There was an emergency door. A few people walked by on the street, but no one seemed to pay any attention to him. He knocked. There was no answer, though he heard a shuffling inside. He knocked again, and the door opened to reveal a short, muscular, dark, hairy man in an undershirt. The man was probably in his late thirties and definitely needed a shave and a bath. His dark hair was thinning rapidly.

"Tsimion Gaidar sent me," Sasha said with a smile.

The man didn't smile back. He examined Tkach, looked at his briefcase, paused, and then backed into the trailer. Sasha ducked his head and followed him. When he got inside, the dark little man pushed the door closed.

The inside of the trailer was one large open space with cabinets along both walls blocking the windows. A bit of light came in from the front and rear windows of the trailer. Both windows were heavily curtained. The metal cabinets, Tkach could see, were padlocked. There was a desk at the rear of the trailer with a chair behind it so the light from outside would come over the shoulder of whoever sat at the desk.

Behind the desk was a second man, who sat with folded hands as if that were the way he contentedly spent all his time. The man behind the desk, wearing a green turtleneck sweater far too warm for the weather, was older than the man who had let Sasha in, but they were obviously related; they had the same sagging face, the same eyes. The older one's hair was white and there was far less of it than there was on the head of his younger relative.

The two men looked at Tkach and waited.

"I'm a student at the university," Tkach said. "I'm a collector of records. Tsimion Gaidar said that you might have one of the Beatles records that went on sale a few months ago at the Melodia record store on Kalinin Prospekt, a Saturday. I waited in line all day. They said there were a hundred thousand of them, but thousands of us were turned away."

The two dark men exchanged glances. The younger

one, standing with his arms folded over his undershirt, shrugged.

Tkach knew far more about the records. Melodia, the Soviet Union's only recording company, had contracted with British EMI to produce 300,000 copies of two Beatles albums originally made in the mid-1960s. Only a few thousand albums were actually made by Melodia, and more than two hundred of those were stolen by a delivery truck driver who was a distant relative of Tsimion Gaidar.

"We might know where to get one of these albums," the older man behind the desk said. His voice was slightly raspy, as if he had just been awakened from a long, deep sleep.

"But," said his younger partner, "it is not cheap."

"I want it very badly," said Tkach.

"Thirty rubles," said the older man.

"Or fifty dollars American," said the younger man.

The older man behind the desk sighed and said, "You must forgive my brother. Osip has American money on the mind. We had a customer, a student like you, a few weeks ago who had some American money. Who knows how he got it? You don't have American money, do you?"

"No," said Sasha. "I don't."

"See?" said the man behind the desk. "You ask dumb questions sometimes."

"But," said Osip in his undershirt, "I sometimes make us a profit with these dumb questions that don't cost us anything to ask."

"What am I to do with such a partner?" the older man asked Sasha, who had no answer. "He tried, my brother, but . . . You want the album?"

"I want it," said Sasha.

"You've got thirty rubles with you?" asked Osip.

"Yes," said Sasha. Actually, he had almost fifty rubles, the price Assistant Procurator Khabolov thought the album would be.

"Where does a student get money like that to carry around?" asked the older man.

"My father is an architect in Tblisi. I'm studying to be an architect," said Sasha.

"Felix, what's the difference where he gets the money? He's got it," said Osip.

"Ignorance," said Felix with a sigh behind the desk, looking at Sasha for understanding. "I promised our mother I would take care of him, but ignorance is hard to overcome."

"Ignorance," grunted Osip. "Without my ignorance we'd still be sewing women's handbags for a few kopecks."

"You hear that?" Felix asked, shaking his head and pointing a hairy finger at his brother. "You hear that? That is not gratitude."

"I've got to get to a class," Sasha said as the brothers glared at each other. He reached into his jacket pocket, took out his wallet, stepped to the small desk, and began to count out rubles.

The rubles sat on the desk and Sasha opened his briefcase. Felix nodded to Osip, who moved to one of the metal cabinets near the front of the trailer, took out a key chain, and opened the cabinet. Sasha couldn't see inside the cabinet from his angle. Osip removed something from the cabinet, tucked it under his sweating arm, and locked the cabinet.

When he returned to the back of the trailer, he handed the album to Sasha, who took it, smiled as if he had obtained a treasure, and tucked it into his briefcase, closing the clasp carefully.

"Thank you," he said. "Perhaps in the future you might be able to obtain other albums for me?"

"We might," said Felix.

"Yes," agreed Osip. "We might."

"Or videotapes. Do you know someplace where I might be able to get videotapes, or even a machine? Tsimion Gaidar thought you might have some idea."

"No idea," said Felix, looking at his brother, who had seemed about to speak.

"Well," said Sasha with a shrug. "I'll keep looking."

Sasha turned toward the emergency door through which he had come. He was sure the brothers were exchanging glances behind him, making a decision.

"Wait," said Felix.

Sasha turned. Felix was standing now.

"As it happens," he said, "we do deal a bit in videotapes, operate a kind of videoteque, quietly, for special customers, special friends."

"I could use a machine," Sasha said, looking at Felix. "My father gave me an Electrokina VM12, but it isn't very good."

"The Soviet factory is, unfortunately, inferior to those of the West," Felix sighed sympathetically. "Given a bit of time we can get a Korean machine or even American Magnavoxes."

"Five thousand American dollars," Osip said quickly.

"He doesn't have American dollars," Felix rasped.

"And tapes?" Sasha asked before the brothers could launch into another argument.

"American or Japanese blank tapes, sixty rubles," said Felix.

"And that's a bargain," added Osip. "Foreign movies, American, one hundred and twenty rubles. We're not talking about *Potemkin* and *Ivan the Terrible* or biographies of admirals."

The trailer was hot. Sasha felt the sweat under his arms.

"I'm very interested," said Sasha, "but I've got to get to class. I can come back later."

"Show him," Felix said to his brother and nodded at the metal cabinet beside him.

Osip moved to the cabinet, took out his key, and opened the cabinet. On shelves, tightly stacked, stood hundreds of videotapes.

"You understand English?" Osip asked Sasha. Sasha nodded that he did.

"All English and American in this cabinet. Your choice," said Osip proudly. "Everything from *Bambi* to *Blue Thunder*."

Sasha felt his smile disappear just when it should be

expanding. He thought of the book in his briefcase and of the little girl near the trailer, the little girl with the two yellow ribbons who had guided him to the book, the little girl who was probably the daughter of one of these men, both of whom were about to be arrested for an economic crime considered by the Soviet Union to be punishable by death.

THREE

ROSTNIKOV KNOCKED AT ONE OF THE GLASS DOORS OF the New Circus and shaded his eyes to peer into the lobby. Nothing seemed to stir. He knocked again and saw some movement. Behind him thunder cracked, but it was the thunder of a departing storm heading north. What had Duznetzov said before he leaped from the Gogol statue? Something about a man who saw thunder? A face appeared on the other side of the window, the face of an old man with sunken gray cheeks and steely gray hair that wouldn't stay in place. He wore a shiny old blue suit that looked at least two sizes too large.

"*Zakri'ta*, closed," the old man shouted. Then he pointed a bony finger to the right. "*Kah'si*, ticket office."

Rostnikov pulled out his identification card and placed it against the glass. The old man fished out a pair of steel-rimmed glasses, donned them, and opened his mouth to read the card. Enlightenment came suddenly, and the man pushed open the door.

"But the police have already been here," the old man said, stepping back to let Rostnikov enter.

"We are here again," Rostnikov said, looking around the lobby.

"I see. I see," said the old man, folding his hands and looking around for help that didn't come. "I see."

"Good," said Rostnikov.

"You've come about the accident, about Pesknoko. Tragic. Tragic. Tragic."

"And Duznetzov. You know about the death this morning of Valerian Duznetzov?"

"Comrade Valerian," sighed the old man. "Coincidence. Yes. Coincidence. Coincidence. Amazing. Two in the same act in one day. It never happened before. Patnietsko says bad luck comes in threes. I would not like to be Katya. No. I wouldn't want to be Katya."

"Katya?"

"Katya," said the old man with irritation. "You know. Katya."

"Katya?"

"Rashkovskaya."

"The last . . ."

". . . member of the Pesknoko act. Yes."

With this the old man shook his head, looked down, and appeared to be lost in his thoughts.

"When I was a boy," the old man said, still looking down, "my father was an assistant to Lunacharsky. He, my father, called him Anatoly Vasilyvich. That's how close they were. They started the postrevolutionary circus together. I met Gorky. Stanislavsky used to pat me on the head. Right like this. On the head."

With this, the old man reached down and patted the imaginary head of an imaginary boy. Rostnikov imagined his son, Josef, and interrupted. "I'd like to see this Katya Rashkovskaya. Where could I find her? And the circus director?"

"The director?" the old man asked, stepping back. "No. No. No. The director is away, setting up a tour. Been gone for . . . I don't know. Weeks. Perhaps the assistant?"

"An assistant will be fine, Comrade," said Rostnikov, wanting to find someplace to sit. "And Katya?"

"Rashkovskaya, yes. I'll see what I can find. If you'll . . ."

"I'll go into the arena," Rostnikov said, walking to one of the entrance doors.

The old man mumbled something behind him, but Rostnikov kept walking. As he opened the door he heard the old man's footsteps echo away behind him. It was not quite dark inside the arena though the lights were down except in the ring in the center. There was, as in all Russian circuses, only one ring so that all attention could be focused on an individual performance or spectacle.

Two men in the ring were trying to get a pig to do something with a barrel. Rostnikov watched silently for a few moments and then turned and started to walk up a stairway toward the first of two promenade walkways that circled the arena.

Behind him, their voices pleading, demanding, the two men urged the squealing pig to greater effort. It was difficult to pull his reluctant leg up the stairs, but Rostnikov went higher, searching for something. He remembered the lights above the arena, the reflecting lights that resembled a rippling circus tent. He remembered the four huge, evenly spaced screens circling the arena above the wood-paneled walls. He remembered the complex rigging, with clinking metal catching the lights high above like stars. And then, among the 3,400 seats, he found the two he was looking for, the two seats in which he and Josef had sat one night more than a dozen years before.

Rostnikov sat in the seat he thought had been his and looked down at the two men and the pig, who seemed to be getting closer to whatever it was they were trying to do. Rostnikov watched in the semidarkness as one of the two men reached up to grasp a metal bar, suspended from the darkness of the ceiling, and bent backward. Then, suddenly, miraculously, the man kicked his feet upward, where they remained, perpendicular to the ground, defying gravity. The first man placed the pig on the contorted man's outstretched legs, and the pig himself rose on two legs, balanced on the contorted man. Meanwhile, the standing man cooed soothingly to the pig. It was an odd but fascinating sight.

"When we see the back of an individual contorted in fear and bent in humiliation, we cannot but look around and doubt our very existence, fearing lest we lose ourselves. But on seeing a fearless acrobat in bright costume, we forget ourselves, feeling that we have somehow risen above ourselves and reached the level of universal strength. Then we can breathe easier."

Without turning to the deep male voice behind him, Rostnikov said, "Karl Marx."

"Yes, Karl Marx," said the voice. "You are a good Soviet citizen, Comrade."

"I like the circus," Rostnikov answered, still fascinated by the men and the pig.

"That is the Brothers Heuber and their pig, Chuska," said the deep voice. "They are paying homage to the great political satirists Vladimir and Anatoly Durov and their pig, Chuska. Pigs are the smartest of all animals. Not dogs, not horses, not bears, not cats. Pigs."

"Monkeys?" asked Rostnikov without taking his eyes from the act below him.

"Monkeys, perhaps," said the man, moving to sit beside Rostnikov, "but only because they share with us the opposable thumb. You've worked in a circus? No, I'd know you. But you have the arms of a lifter or catcher."

"I lift weights," said Rostnikov as the act in the ring came to a sudden end. The man who had placed the pig on the other's feet grabbed the animal and tucked it under his arm. The perpendicular man eased himself down and the two men strode away talking, arguing, as Rostnikov turned to face the man at his side.

"I am Mazaraki, Dimitri Mazaraki, announcer and assistant to the head of the New Moscow Circus. I used to be a trick lifter. I still do the act occasionally, but my back is not so certain as it was. Now I cannot hold up twelve young women on a platform all representing a year in a new agricultural plan, all dressed as different grains. No, now I can only do five-year plans."

Rostnikov took the man's hand. It was, like the man himself, strong, firm. Mazaraki was wearing a perfectly pressed light gray suit with a one-color black tie. Standing, he would be half a head taller than Rostnikov. He was about Rostnikov's weight and about ten years younger, perhaps forty. He had a billowing black mustache and dark wavy hair with a white streak on the left temple. Most impressive were his bearing, his straight back, his muscles straining against his suit.

Rostnikov wondered if Mazaraki's white streak looked like the white streak of Cotton Hawes in the 87th Precinct novels. For a moment he couldn't quite remember on which side Hawes's white streak was, only that it had been caused by a knife.

". . . as it usually is," Mazaraki said.

"I'm sorry," said Rostnikov. "I was thinking."

"I said," Mazaraki said with a weary grin, "the circus is not as busy today as it usually is. The accident. Yaro said you were here about the accident?"

"It may not have been an accident," said Rostnikov, watching Mazaraki's face.

Mazaraki smiled as if he were being told a joke. Then he realized it was no joke.

"Not an . . ."

"Perhaps," Rostnikov said with a shrug. "Who knows? First one partner leaps from a statue and at the same time another accidentally dies in a fall. It could be a coincidence."

"The officer who came earlier . . ." Mazaraki began.

". . . did not know of Duznetzov and his flight from Gogol's head," finished the inspector. "I haven't been to the circus for a dozen years."

Mazaraki was probably confused, which was fine with Rostnikov.

"The safety net did not hold, is that correct?" asked Rostnikov, looking down at where the net would be during a performance.

"That's right," said Mazaraki, adjusting his lapels, which needed no adjustment. "We have the best support crew in the world, the best, but Oleg may have tried to adjust the net himself. Maybe . . ."

"Maybe," agreed Rostnikov with a sigh, standing up. "I should like to talk to the surviving partner, Katya Rashkovskaya."

"She's not here," said Mazaraki. "We sent her home. This was difficult for all of us, but for her it is—it is devastating."

"Yes," agreed Rostnikov, resisting the urge to massage his leg for the trip back down the stairs he should not have climbed. "Duznetzov drank?"

"Yes," said Mazaraki, standing. He was even taller than Rostnikov had guessed, not quite a giant, but a man to be looked at twice on the street. "Valerian Duznetzov was fond of vodka."

"Did he say strange things when he was drunk?" asked Rostnikov, starting down the stairs. A new act had begun to take over the ring for rehearsal; a wire was being strung about a dozen feet from the ground. The four gray-uniformed attendants moved quickly, quietly, efficiently, while a man and woman in zippered sweat suits waited patiently for them to finish.

"We all say strange things when we are drunk. It is the nature of being drunk. Would you like to stay and watch for a while, Inspector . . ."

"Rostnikov. No, I would like to be given the address of Katya Rashkovskaya."

"You say Valerian said strange things before he—he jumped from the statue. What strange things?"

"He said he could fly and he could teach me to fly to other countries if I had the money. And he seemed to be afraid of a man who saw thunder."

"That makes no sense," said Mazaraki.

Rostnikov shrugged and continued down the steps.

"Does a pig balanced on the feet of an acrobat make sense?" Rostnikov asked.

"Yes," Mazaraki said, laughing, as he followed behind him. "It all makes sense. The pig is a figure of the farm economy, delicately balanced to serve the needs of the people by the skill of the Soviet farmer, who can juggle, balance, perform near-miracles of skill. It also demonstrates the level of specialized skill Soviet society can nurture, admire, and protect."

"It is fascinating," said Rostnikov, coming to the arena exit door. "But it makes little sense."

He turned to face the larger man, who worried his mustache with his fingers and cautiously examined this rather strange policeman. Then the bigger man grinned and shook his head as he whispered, "Perhaps you are right, but it would be just as well to protect illusions. The illusions of adults are as important as the illusions of children. I trust that this conversation is between us alone."

"Your trust is safe," said Rostnikov, turning for a glance at the young woman who was climbing up to the wire. She began to bounce gingerly, her breasts rippling under the sweat suit.

"It can't hurt for you to watch for a minute or two," said Mazaraki.

"Well," said Rostnikov, "perhaps for a minute or two."

The two men turned and watched the act from the darkness of the entranceway, and Rostnikov thought that it would not hurt to see Katya Rashkovskaya a little later, to eat a little later, to get home a little later tonight, to talk to Sarah about Josef's posting to Afghanistan a little later tonight. His eyes moved to the young woman, who balanced, turned to the voice of the man who stood below her, and Rostnikov felt for an instant as if the woman were moving in slow motion.

Precisely at noon, according to the clock on his desk, Emil Karpo placed the pen he was writing with in line with the two other identical pens on his desk and got up from his chair. He walked to the small sink in the corner of the room, filled his teakettle with water, prepared his cup, and started the hot plate, on which he placed the kettle. He took a neatly wrapped half-loaf of grainy dark bread from the cabinet under the table on which the hot plate stood, tore off a large piece of the bread, placed it on the plate that held the waiting teacup, and stood facing the wall over his bed. He began the exercises he had been taught to strengthen his left hand, began counting as he opened, closed, twisted, tensed, relaxed. He finished the last exercise within three seconds of the water's boiling.

Karpo removed the teakettle using his right hand, prepared his tea, and sat at the small table near the window to eat. He considered raising the window shade but decided against it, against the distraction that daylight might cause. He ate slowly, chewing fully, drinking in small sips, not allowing himself to think, concentrating on the patterns of grain in the bread, the particles of tea in the dark bottom of his cup. Emil Karpo never ate at the same table at which he worked and he never thought about his work when he ate. It wasn't because he enjoyed eating. Emil Karpo neither enjoyed nor disliked it. He knew his body; his sense of taste responded to ice cream, a fact that caused him to avoid eating ice cream as an act of discipline. No, he ate away from his desk because he believed his mind needed cleansing, respite.

Following the meal, Karpo cleaned his cup and plate in the sink, set them out to dry, and then stepped behind his desk chair, on which he placed his palms, and closed his eyes. Images came. He thrust them aside, ordered them to go without words, and they went. Words came. He banished them as well. When they were gone, he banished thinking about them and for what seemed but an instant Karpo heard only the possibility of a hum and saw only the faint hint of roundness. When he opened his eyes, he saw by the clock that he had been meditating for almost an hour.

Karpo sat at his desk and reviewed what he had. The eight cases appeared to have their means of death in common: multiple stabbing, lower abdomen, pelvic area. The number of penetrations varied from seven to sixteen. The depth of the plunges was similar. The blade, according to the report by the medical laboratory technician Paulinin, was the same one in all cases. Paulinin had concluded that the killer was a man, probably reasonably large and strong.

Beyond this, little was evident. The murders were generally in places where prostitutes could be found—a few bars on Gorky Street, near the railway stations—but there seemed to be no pattern. Two in a row were in the Riga Station area. Three were within two blocks of the Yaroslavl Station, but they weren't consecutive. There were no murders near any of the other seven railway stations. And there was no pattern to the specific sites. Twice the killer struck in doorways. Once in a women's public toilet. The deliveryway to the Marx and Engels Museum another time. The period between murders formed no pattern. It varied from months to days. Even the time of day established little other than that the murderer probably had a job with normal day hours, since all of the murders took place in the late evening—with one exception. The second prostitute, Hild Grachovnaya, had been murdered on a Tuesday afternoon, which might or might not have meant that Tuesday was the killer's day off. The women had nothing in common other than that they were prostitutes. Some were young. Some not so young. One was a Ukrainian. Another was a Mongol.

The charts in front of him looked random, and Karpo knew that a further complication might be that there were other victims about which he knew nothing. There were a few missing prostitutes. But that meant little. They might even be dead, but it didn't prove that this serial killer had murdered them. It might also be that he didn't kill only prostitutes, that he killed other women, men, boys, children, in a different manner, that the victims dictated the way they would be killed. That might account for the misfiled report. It had been in the file along with the others. Karpo had carefully copied every word. He had his copy before him, but it made little sense. It was in the file for this killer, but it had the wrong file number, at least it had originally had the wrong file number. Someone had carefully crossed out the old number and typed in the number of this case.

There had been a number of people investigating the murders; each one was listed on the enclosed reports, along

with Anatoly Vidbraki, who had been assigned the entire
series a year ago, just before he dropped dead of a heart
attack. There had been a murder since then—two, if one
counted the killing recounted in the renumbered report.
Karpo reread his copy of the report on the murder of Sonia
Melyodska. It had been a stabbing but with a different
knife from all the others. The murderer had stabbed only
twice and much deeper than in the other killings. The killing had been in the daytime, which was not necessarily out
of the pattern, but the victim had definitely not been a
prostitute. She had been a soldier in uniform on leave, and
she was killed on the stairway in the Vdnkh Metro Station.
The killing was even witnessed by an old woman who saw
only that the killer was a heavy man who fled up the stairs.

Normally, Emil Karpo would have simply examined the
report and determined that the investigating officer had
made a mistake, in this case a very big mistake. That was
not uncommon. Though it displeased him, Karpo had long
since learned to accept incompetence and lack of dedication among the police, as he had learned to accept it among
shop clerks, street cleaners, office workers, everyone.
There was nothing wrong with the various economic and
revolutionary plans that had been put forth to move the
Soviet Union forward. The problem lay in the lack of discipline of the people, not all the people, but too many
people: the very old, who were corrupted by memories of
life before the revolution, and the young, who were corrupted with visions of tempting sloth in France and the
United States.

The weakness of the people, the corruption of the system, were not peculiar to the Russians. Karpo was sure of
that. Triumph, vindication, for communism would not ultimately begin with the masses. It never had. It would begin
with the few who were dedicated, were willing to sacrifice,
to take on the burden and serve as silent examples. Lenin
had done this.

But this apparently misfiled report was not a sign of
weakness and mistake. Porfiry Petrovich Rostnikov had
written this report, had conducted the investigation of the

murder of Corporal Sonia Melyodska in the Vdnkh Metro Station. In many ways Rostnikov was a puzzle to Emil Karpo. In many ways Rostnikov, with his unstated criticism of the state, was a challenge to Emil Karpo. But Rostnikov did not make big mistakes like this. In investigations, Rostnikov seldom made any mistakes at all. He moved carefully, slowly, sometimes too slowly, but he did not make mistakes.

The solution was simple. Karpo turned off his desk lamp, stood up, and went to look for Rostnikov.

At the moment Emil Karpo left his small room and carefully set on the door the tiny hair that would betray an intruder, Sasha Tkach was sitting in the office of the assistant procurator for the Moscow district. Procurator Khabolov's hound dog face was sniffing the report Sasha had written on the Gorgasali brothers, Felix and Osip, the black market dealers in videotapes and records. It didn't seem important enough to Sasha for him to be called right to the assistant procurator's office. It was a large, bare office with a desk in the middle of the wooden floor, a pair of large windows behind the desk, and a photograph of Lenin between the windows. Sasha Tkach had been in this office very few times. He did not enjoy his visits. He would have felt more comfortable clutching the briefcase on his lap, but he kept his hands resting gently on it as he watched Khabolov's face.

Assistant Procurator Khabolov, on the other hand, greatly enjoyed the visits of junior investigators. Khabolov had been in his current position for less than a year, having replaced Anna Timofeyeva, who had put in ten years without a vacation and had worked eighteen-hour days and six-and-a-half-day weeks during that decade until the moment of her first heart attack. Khabolov was determined that he would meet no such fate. As dedicated as Anna Timofeyeva had been to her job, Khabolov was dedicated to Khabolov.

He pretended to read the report one more time, slowly, watching Tkach out of the corner of his eyes. Some of the older, more experienced inspectors were less impressed by Khabolov's act. Their visits were not visits he enjoyed. Little was known about Khabolov among the staff of the Procurator's Office, but he was not viewed as a man of mystery. Most knew enough and guessed the rest after spending ten minutes with him.

Khabolov had no training in law. He had come to his first term as a deputy procurator after having distinguished himself as a ferret who sniffed out shirkers among factory workers. His moment of glory had come when he discovered the tunnel in an Odessa piston factory through which workers were smuggling vodka, which they consumed in great quantities, leading to a slowing down of production and a failure to meet quotas. Khabolov had later, through the payment of strategic bribes, discovered how a trio of dock workers had funneled Czech toothpaste into the black market. He had been rewarded for his many revelations with the job he now held.

"Mmm," Khabolov hummed, eyes still fixed on the report. His hand went up to the top button of his brown uniform. He unbuttoned the button and sat back, reaching for the now-tepid cup of tea in front of him.

Sasha Tkach knew enough to show nothing.

Khabolov finished his tea, put down the cup, looked at the report, placed it on the empty desk, and patted it with his hand. Only then did he look at Tkach.

"*Fartsoushchiki*," he said with contempt. "Black marketers. You can smell them."

The deputy procurator's nostrils curled as if he were smelling one of the Gorgasali brothers.

"You've done well. This is a good report. You've returned the twenty rubles you did not spend?"

"Yes, Comrade," Tkach said quickly.

"And the record album?"

"Here, in my briefcase," Tkach said, snapping open the case and reaching in. His hands found the wrapped copy of the children's book he had bought for Pulcharia, moved under it, and came out with *A Hard Day's Night*.

Khabolov didn't move.

"I can . . ." Tkach began.

"Leave it right here," Khabolov said, his hands folded on the desk, his eyes on Tkach.

Tkach put the album on the edge of the desk. Khabolov ignored it.

"This is an important black market operation, Comrade Tkach," the deputy said, leaning forward, his voice dropping. "Perhaps not as important as the automobile thieves you were instrumental in catching, but quite important."

Since Khabolov seemed to be waiting for a response, Tkach said, "Yes, Comrade."

"Quite important," Khabolov repeated, as if something were now understood between them. "They have other connections, these brothers of yours. That is certain. We can bring them in now or we can take this investigation to the next step, to find out who supplies these brothers, these traitors to the five-year plan."

Again Khabolov waited.

"What is the next step, Comrade?" Tkach asked.

"I will personally visit these two thieves who deserve to be prosecuted, deserve to be shot," Khabolov said, his hand reaching out to touch the Beatles album on the corner of the desk. "I have experience in situations like this, black market rings like this. I have worked closely with the KGB, very closely. This can serve as an important learning experience for you."

"Thank you, Comrade Procurator," Tkach said.

"For the time being," Khabolov went on, opening his desk drawer and sliding both Sasha's report and the album into it, "we will keep this investigation quiet. When we have the entire ring, you will be given full credit."

"Thank you, Comrade," said Tkach.

"Good, good. That will be all for now," said Khabolov, retrieving a file from another drawer. "You have other cases. Get back to them and I'll let you know when this one needs your attention."

With this Khabolov's wet eyes turned to the new report, and Sasha strode to the door and out into the hall.

Tkach checked the lock on his briefcase, took in a deep

breath, and hurried to the Petrovka elevator. He wasn't sure if Deputy Khabolov took him for a fool or for a young man wise enough to play the fool. He wasn't at all sure how clever Deputy Procurator Khabolov was. He might be playing a role, setting Tkach up.

The elevator door opened and Tkach entered. Two women in the rear were talking to a man Tkach recognized from the criminal records room in the basement. Tkach nodded at Pon, and Pon adjusted his glasses and nodded back as the elevator doors closed.

Tkach was quite sure what he was going to do. He was going to forget the video pirates and get back to his other cases. He was going to forget the video pirates and let the deputy procurator do whatever he planned to do. All he wanted to do now was finish out the day and get home to his wife and daughter with his gift.

The elevator stopped at the fifth floor and Tkach got out.

"It's been a hard day's night," he said to himself and smiled, but it wasn't a smile of mirth.

"What are you smiling about, you soggy bear?" Nikolai asked as Yuri entered the apartment on Galushkina Street.

Yuri had not been aware that he was smiling. He had nothing particularly to smile about, less now that he could see that Nikolai was drunk again. Nikolai was a near-dwarf of a man who always needed a shave and was forever brushing back his hair, which, when he was drunk, was somehow always wet. Also, when he was drunk, Nikolai's cheeks puffed out as if he had just returned from having his wisdom teeth removed. Nikolai looked like a chipmunk with bad teeth.

"I'm not smiling," Yuri said, putting down the briefcase he always carried—not because he needed it for work, but because it was a sign that he worked in an office, that he was someone important enough to have written work to bring home. It was also very handy for carrying the knife.

"He's not smiling," Nikolai said to the ceiling. "I can't tell when a man is smiling. I'm losing my eyesight."

Yuri moved to the tiny refrigerator in the corner, and Nikolai had to turn in his chair to watch his roommate remove a bottle of watered fruit juice.

"You're supposed to mix that with something," Nikolai said. "You drink that stuff without alcohol and it can give you an ulcer. My—"

"Why are you home?" Yuri asked, adjusting his glasses and pouring himself a glass of fruit drink.

"Why? Listen to him. I live here. I sleep on that bed under the sink in which I wash and shave and from which I drink. That sink. Why am I? What kind of question—?"

"You don't get off work for two hours," Yuri said, still standing, as he sipped the drink and let himself look around the filthy room. When Nikolai passed out, which might be in hours or minutes, Yuri would clean it up. Yuri didn't like things messy, out of place. Sanity dictated that Yuri should not like Nikolai, but like him he did, or, perhaps, need him was a better way to put it. They were used to each other. They were a wall against loneliness.

Nikolai talked of women, said obscene things, even suggested that he went to prostitutes, but Yuri doubted it. Nikolai was as doomed to be what he was as Yuri Pon was resolved to be what he had become. What it was that Yuri had become was not easy to define. Yuri walked to the window with his drink and looked down at the street below as Nikolai explained.

"I became ill at the factory. My vision clouded. My eyes began to water. My ears began to ring. The voices of dead socialist poets began to call my name. A terrible fever came over me."

"And now?" Yuri asked after finishing his drink.

"I'm fine!" shouted Nikolai, gulping down the last of the clear liquid in his glass. "It's a miracle. If there were a God, this would prove his existence. We should celebrate my miraculous recovery."

Nikolai stood, swayed, and made for the bottle on the table.

"A few more illnesses at the factory and you'll lose your job," said Yuri, moving to the sink to wash his glass. "Article Sixty of the Constitution of the Union of Soviet Socialist Republics states that it is the duty of, and a matter of honor for, every able-bodied citizen of the USSR to work conscientiously in his chosen, socially useful, occupation, and to strictly observe labor discipline. Evasion of socially useful work is incompatible with the principles of socialist society."

"If I lose this job I'll find another," said Nikolai, grinning and walking toward his roommate with a fresh drink in hand.

"You're drunk." Yuri sighed, shaking his hands to dry them.

"Yes, but it used to be more fun to be drunk," said Nikolai. "Now it's a crime to be drunk. Gorbachev tells us that drunkenness is an affront to the state, an unwillingness to face the harshness of reality, to cope with our problems. He is a wise man."

"A wise man," agreed Yuri, humoring Nikolai, who drank deeply without taking his eyes from the taller man.

"But a cruel one, soggy bear," said Nikolai. "It is cruel to force us to remain sober. What have we to turn to for our imaginations, to release our inhabitants—"

"Inhibitions," Yuri corrected, moving to the table.

"Inhibitions," agreed Nikolai.

The two men sat facing each other silently across the table as if something profound had just been said.

"You don't drink," Nikolai suddenly accused. "You don't go to movies. You don't go to museums. You don't watch television. We don't have a television. We can't afford a television. And the news, the news is, is . . ."

"Zakuski," Yuri supplied.

"Zakuski, yes. Hors d'oeuvres. You don't even talk about women. I'll tell you," and with this he pointed a finger in Yuri's face, "you've never even been with a woman."

This time Yuri Pon did smile.

"What? Why are you smiling? I said something funny?" Nikolai asked in mock confusion. "The bear has a harem somewhere? Another luxury apartment, perhaps a little wooden *izbas* in the country where you bring women and have wild orgies? If I thought that were true and you didn't invite me, it could well be the end of our . . . You sure you don't want to join me?" With this, Nikolai held up his sloshing glass as an offering. "It is not as much fun to drink alone, you know. It's fun, but not as much."

"I can't drink tonight," Yuri said. "I've got to go out shopping."

Nikolai slouched back and laughed like a horse.

"Going to look for a woman, eh, Yuri?"

"Perhaps, yes."

"And what are you going to do with her, Yuri? You want to bring her back here?"

"No," said Pon. "No."

"You should be a comedian," said Nikolai, laughing. "A funny comedian. I don't think," he chuckled, leaning forward and whispering, "that you would know what to do with a woman."

"I know what to do with a woman," Pon said.

"You want me to come with you and help?" Nikolai said, unable to control his mirth.

"No," said Pon softly. "I won't need any help."

FOUR

THE GUNSHOT CAME JUST AS ROSTNIKOV PUSHED OPEN
the door to the seventh floor of the high rise on Lenin
Prospekt about four blocks from the New Circus. In spite
of his leg, he had purposely taken a circuitous route to the
address of Katya Rashkovskaya. It had been a year or more
since he had roamed this neighborhood. So Rostnikov had
wandered up Lenin Prospekt, watching the people shop,
looking into the windows of the elegantly decorated shops,
passing the Varna (which specialized in products from Bul-
garia), the Vlasta (with goods from Czechoslovakia), and
the Leipzig (with exports from the German Democratic
Republic). Rostnikov bought nothing. He had limped along
without putting words to his thoughts, paused to examine a
window of shoes that would cost at least a month of his
salary, ignored a quarrel between two men over a parking
space near Lumumba Friendship University, and gradually
made his way to the second of three white-concrete high
rises.

He had trudged his way up the stairs in the elevatorless
building, moving slowly to minimize perspiration. On the
seventh floor he had paused for breath before opening the

hallway door. That was when he heard the shot. It wasn't that Rostnikov didn't believe in coincidence. If one lived long enough, particularly in Moscow, one encountered all manner of coincidence. Cases were often closed through coincidence rather than hard work. An officer happened to see a car thief breaking into a car when it looked as if a particular ring of thieves would never be caught. The officer was not staking out the street, was not even on duty, but had taken a wrong turn looking for a movie theater that, as it turned out, was on the other side of Moscow.

In this case, however, when he heard the shot, Porfiry Petrovich did not assume that he had been fortunate or unfortunate enough to step onto the scene of a crime at the coincidental moment. He hobbled as quickly as he could in search of apartment 717. Here a door opened and a cautious eye peeped out. There a door opened quickly and closed. Beyond, a man in a robe, who looked as if he slept days and worked nights, stepped into the hall rubbing his eyes and almost running into Rostnikov, who barreled past him and found apartment 717.

There was a voice behind the door, a hysterical voice that might have been wailing wordlessly or might have been saying something. Rostnikov turned to the sleepy man in the robe, who looked puzzled, and said, "Call Petrovka thirty-eight. Tell them Inspector Rostnikov told you to call. Say it's a possible shooting."

The man nodded and hurried back into his apartment, where, Rostnikov hoped, he had a phone and was not simply going back to bed. Rostnikov pounded on the door once, hard. The door vibrated.

"Police. Open the door," he said, loud but calm.

Nothing happened inside, though he thought he heard the sound of something, an appliance, something, above the wailing voice.

"Open or I'll have to break the door," Rostnikov said, still calm.

Footsteps moved quickly inside and the door opened to reveal a thin young man in a blue T-shirt. His straight blond hair looked bleached and was combed back from his smooth and wide-eyed face.

"I told her not to," the young man said, stepping back to admit Rostnikov. "I told her it was stupid. That there were other things she could—"

"Where?" said Rostnikov, grabbing the young man's arm. "Where is she?"

The young man groaned in pain, twisted his body, and pointed toward a closed door across the room. Rostnikov let him go and hurried to the door. Behind the door was the sound he had heard in the hall, the appliance sound. He pushed the door open and found himself facing a quite beautiful woman of about thirty with a pistol in her hand. Her straight black hair was long, and tied behind her head with a yellow ribbon. She was wearing a yellow skirt and blouse and white sneakers. The gun was aimed directly at Rostnikov and looked none too secure in her grip.

"Who?" she shrieked, backing up.

"Police," he said, keeping his voice down but still audible above the rushing mechanical sound in the small bathroom. "You'd better give me the gun."

Katya Rashkovskaya looked down at the gun in her hand as if she had not expected to see it there. She handed it instantly to Rostnikov, who dropped it into his pocket. Behind him, Rostnikov could hear the young blond man move to the open doorway of the small room.

"What did you try to do?" Rostnikov asked, gently reaching out to touch the young woman's arm. He had dealt with attempted suicides before, both those who succeeded and those who failed. His theories were different from the party line. His theories were based on experience. It was Rostnikov's belief that all but a very small, insignificant number meant to kill themselves, even the ones who later said and believed that they had only been acting out or pretending. It was, he guessed, like childbirth as Sarah had described it. When it is happening, it is terrible and real. When it is over, it is like a dream. A similarity between the bringing of life and the taking of it.

"She shot the toilet!" the young man cried behind him.

Rostnikov turned and looked at the nearly hysterical young man and then at the young woman, who looked as if she had been hypnotized. And then he looked at the toilet, and, indeed, there was a crack in the porcelain, starting with a hole the size of a blintz and zigzagging out into a series of tributaries. Behind the hole, the toilet gurgled loudly and angrily.

"It's true?" Rostnikov asked, moving closer to the young woman.

She nodded her head slowly, indicating that it was true. Rostnikov nodded back and led her out of the bathroom past the young man, who backed away.

"Close the door," Rostnikov ordered. The young man closed the bathroom door, which cut back on but did not end the noise. After leading the woman to a chair and being sure she sat, Rostnikov pulled a straight-backed chair over and sat facing her. He took her hand and said, "I understand."

She looked at his face, expecting to see a lie, but saw instead that this man, whoever he was, this clothed trunk of a man with a flat face, did seem to understand, which puzzled Katya Rashkovskaya, who wasn't at all sure whether she understood what she had done. One minute she had been sitting in grief and anger over the deaths of Oleg and Valerian. Eugene, her brother, had been talking about himself. She had been drinking tea. And then the idea had come. No, it was not quite an idea. She hated the toilet. It had caused them, the three of them, nothing but trouble. Oleg had tried to get the building supervisor to fix it, had gone to the neighborhood party deputy in charge, had tried to bribe, beg, threaten, but nothing had helped.

And so, sitting there, vaguely hearing the voice of her brother suggest that now that she was alone in this large apartment he could move in, she had suddenly risen, gone to Valerian's drawer, moved the shirts he would never again wear, and pulled out the gun. The next thing she knew this sympathetic man with the face and body of a bear had gently told her that he understood.

"She's gone mad!" the young man cried, pacing back

and forth. "All this death has driven her mad."

"Are you mad?" Rostnikov asked Katya. She shook her head no.

"She says she is not mad," Rostnikov reported.

"She says!" the young man cried in disbelief.

"I believe her," said the inspector.

"You . . ."

"Who are you?" Rostnikov asked, still holding the woman's hand but looking at the man.

"I, I don't have to tell you who I am," the young man said.

"Yes, you do," Rostnikov said sadly. "I'm the police."

The word *police* did nothing to the woman, but it froze the young man.

"I'm Eugene Rashkovsky, Katya's brother. I came to help her in her grief. She—"

"He's a *nakhlebnik*, a parasite," Katya said. "He came to move into the apartment. He was afraid to come here when Oleg was . . . here. Oleg would throw him out. Oleg didn't like young men who—"

"You've no reason to start that again!" Eugene screamed. "No reason." He looked at Rostnikov in fear and hurried to his sister. "That has nothing to do with the police, nothing."

"Go," Katya said, reaching up with her free hand to wipe away hair that had not fallen in front of her eyes.

"I . . ." Eugene began.

"Go," Rostnikov repeated, and Eugene stormed out of the apartment, slamming the door behind him.

When he was gone, Rostnikov said, "I know a lot about toilets."

"Yes," Katya said, a sad smile touching her mouth. "You are the police."

"No, I don't mean that metaphorically. I'm not talking about crime. I'm talking about toilets. I could never get the apparatus to fix my toilet, so I learned to do it myself, to fix it myself. I was determined. I borrowed tools, found people who knew people who knew people who could get me parts. I learned. I think I even know a place where you can get a toilet bowl. You want to learn to repair your own toilet, I'll let you borrow my books."

Katya pulled her hand away slowly and folded both hands on her lap.

"I thought that was forbidden. That you could not repair your own plumbing. You're a policeman."

"Fixing a toilet is a challenge," Rostnikov said, sitting back to give her a bit more room. "It is something that gives you a sense of triumph when you get it done in spite of what it takes to do it."

"Maybe I'll borrow your books," she said. "Would you like some tea?"

"Tea would be nice," Rostnikov said. He watched her stand up and move across the large room to the open kitchen. He turned in his chair to watch her.

"I'd like—" he began, but was interrupted by the door's bursting open. An MVD officer in uniform leaped in, gun in hand, unsure of whether he should aim his weapon at the young woman who seemed to be making tea or at the older man sitting in the chair. He chose the man in the chair.

"Don't move!" the officer shouted.

"I'm Inspector Rostnikov." Rostnikov sighed, glancing at Katya, who went on making the tea. "And you are?"

"Vadim Malkoliovich Dunin," said the young man, who appeared to Rostnikov to be no more than twelve years old.

"How old are you?"

"How? I am twenty-four," the policeman answered.

"Vadim Malkoliovich, put away your gun and leave. Wait in the hall. Let no one in unless I allow it."

"But I was told—"

"A mistake. I have everything under control. Leave. And close the door behind you if it will close. How long have you been in uniform?"

The young officer looked confused as he holstered his gun. "Four months."

"Advice," said Rostnikov. "Always knock. It often happens that the worst part of a domestic problem results from the attempts by people involved to get repairs done for the damage caused by the police who had come to help them."

"I'm sorry, Comrade Inspector, but . . . If there is anything I can do?"

"Can you fix broken doors?"

"No, I don't think so."

"Then learn to do so or stop breaking them."

"Yes, Comrade Inspector," the young man said, backing out. He closed the door behind him and it stayed reasonably closed.

Katya returned with the tea: a cup for Rostnikov, one for herself. She sat, gave him sugar. They said nothing for a few minutes as they drank and listened to the muffled sound of the toilet.

"I have been assigned to investigate the deaths of your partners," he said, finishing his tea and placing the cup and saucer on a white cloth on a little table nearby. "I was with Valerian Duznetzov when he died this morning."

Katya looked up from her tea and bit her lower lip.

"You were, you were there when he fell?"

"He didn't fall, Katya. He jumped. It was suicide. He was drunk. I think he had been drinking a bit to get up his courage. But it was suicide."

"Oleg didn't commit suicide," she said evenly, looking into his eyes for the first time.

"It doesn't seem so," Rostnikov agreed.

And he saw an awareness cross her face like a slap.

"You think, you think someone might have killed him?"

"My superior, Colonel Snitkonoy, thinks it is a curiosity, a coincidence, two performers in the same act falling to their death in the same morning."

"It could be a terrible coincidence," Katya said, putting down her cup and leaning forward urgently.

"Yes," he said and considered telling the story of the policeman and the car thief.

"What would convince him that it wasn't just a coincidence?" she asked, as if there were an answer she wanted Rostnikov to give but she did not want to hear. Since the idea of something beyond accident had been introduced, Katya Rashkovskaya's pretty face had been touched by fear.

Rostnikov shrugged, puffed out his cheeks, and blew.

"If the third member of the same act died in the same day, is that what you were thinking?" she asked, searching his eyes for an answer.

Her eyes were a magnificent blue. Rostnikov did not really want to frighten her, but it was the fastest way to get information. He could comfort her later, let her borrow his plumbing books, provide her with protection.

"Duznetzov said some strange things before he died," said Rostnikov. "He talked of birds and people flying over walls, of men seeing thunder. He was afraid."

"You said he was drunk," Katya countered, clearly growing afraid herself.

"Drunk and afraid and brave. I liked him."

"He could be very funny," Katya said, folding her arms in front of her and turning her back to Rostnikov.

"Who would want to kill your friends?" he asked.

Her head went down, as did her voice.

"I don't know."

But it was clear to Rostnikov that she did know, or thought she knew.

"You know," he said.

She turned defiantly, ready to argue, her arms still folded closely to her breasts. But her defiance faded as she looked at Rostnikov.

"You think I might be . . ."

"Since I don't know what is happening, I don't know what might or might not happen to you." He got up awkwardly, as he always did when he sat for more than a few minutes, but he managed not to wince in pain. "I don't know what to do to protect you with certainty other than to locate and punish the person who might be responsible for what happened to your friends today."

"But an accident, a suicide, there's no crime," she said as he walked past her toward the door.

"There is a crime before these crimes, a crime sufficient to justify murder. Katya Rashkovskaya, I think you may be in danger. Do you remember my name?"

"Rostnikov," she said. "Inspector Rostnikov."

"When you want to talk to me, call Petrovka thirty-eight or tell the officer who broke your door. He will stay with you for a few days and find a way to fix your door. Can he sleep in here somewhere?"

"I've two extra beds now," she said. "Thank you. Are you, are you really a policeman?"

"Yes," he said.

"You don't talk like a policeman," she said.

"Ah," replied Rostnikov, "the genre is not dictated by the expectation. Each individual within the genre defines it. I am a policeman and, therefore, I must now be incorporated into your concept of a policeman."

"You don't talk like a policeman," she repeated emphatically.

In the hall, Rostnikov found the young policeman, who snapped to attention.

"Vadim Malkoliovich Dunin," he said, "you are to remain with the young woman in this apartment until you are relieved. Find a phone on this floor, call in, and tell your commander that you have been placed on special assignment by me. Do you live nearby?"

"Well . . ." began Dunin.

"Is there someone who can bring you a toothbrush, a change of socks, shorts?"

"My father works at the All-Union Central Council of Trade Unions, which—"

"Good, good. Have him bring you clothes in the morning. Pay Comrade Rashkovskaya for any food she gives you and put in for reimbursement. I'll sign your accounting. You understand all this?"

"No, Comrade," Dunin said.

"You don't have to. Most police work is doing what you are told and not worrying about what it means. Someone may be trying to kill that very pretty young woman and we don't want that to happen."

"No, Comrade."

"Keep yourself busy by trying to fix the door you broke and call me immediately if she says she wants to talk to me. Call me and find me. You understand?"

"I understand," said Dunin. "Fix the door, don't let anyone kill her, and call you if she wants to speak to you."

"Excellent," said Rostnikov, who limped slowly down
the hall as he reached back into his pocket for his notebook.

Someone had to be found to replace the aerialists, Pesknoko and Duznetzov, and, possibly, something would have
to be done about Katya. That could wait, but not for long.
If she met with an accident too soon the police, that barrel-
shaped inspector, would not easily accept the possibility of
coincidence. There might, however, be no choice for him.
There was much to be done and too much to lose. It was
now very dangerous for him to have Katya alive. He could
do it without her.

He had worked all of this out, had found the list of
replacement acts sent by the Soyuzgostsirk, the Central
Circus Administration, and had decided to make a visit to
the Moscow Circus School, officially called the State University of Circus and Stage Acts, where all three of the
new acts in which he was interested were currently training. He had called the school and had been assured that all
three acts would be at the school that afternoon, that all
three were being reviewed, and that a decision would be
made within an hour or two so that the New Circus could
continue its present show without a break.

He crossed in front of Petrovka Park and hurried down
Yamskoipola Street and into the lobby of the school, where
the sounds of acts in preparation and rehearsal came
through the open gym door across the lobby. Built in the
early 1920s immediately after the revolution, the Circus
School remained the single most prestigious source of
circus performers. The building itself, however, showed
distinct signs of mildew and decay. The floorboards in the
lobby were warped, the wallboards were sagged and buckled.

He passed through the museumlike arcade of pillars
covered with historic photographs and moved down the
corridor of classrooms. Ten black-uniformed children sat in

one classroom with the door open. The instructor, a woman with thick glasses, was writing something on the black-board.

He strode on past the rows of photographs of circus performers from almost every country in the world without pausing. He had seen them before, hundreds, thousands, of times. He had been a student here, one of eighty twelve-year-olds accepted his year from three thousand applicants. He had been accepted because his father had been one of the original performers in Lunacharsky's first official Soviet Circus. It wasn't that he wasn't talented, capable, but he knew that he was no more so than hundreds who had been turned down. At the age of twelve he had been given the guarantee of a job for life.

At first he had enjoyed the attention, the prestige. But as the years passed, he began to resent, resent the tricks he was taught, resent the act the teachers decided was right for him. His father had been a magician, an honored magician. The son had begun as a magician, had been moved into developing an act as a magician clown, and ended as an acrobatic clown in an act with three others. It was clear before he left the school that he would never be a star, a truth that was unacceptable to him.

He hurried up the stairs to the second level. Classrooms and offices ringed the outside of the second floor, while the middle of the building was open, looking down on the noisy gym where music played, acts rehearsed, and the retired performers who served as faculty urged students on to hurried perfection. He had arrived in time. He stepped back into the shadows to watch the three acts that were being given a final review by the headmaster and staff. The death of a performer in one of the Soviet circuses was not unusual, and the call for a quick replacement was part of the routine. Lists were constantly being re-vised, acts reviewed, decisions made based on location of the circus, political interest, the kind of act that might be needed, and the possible competition. While the most prestigious acts came from the Circus School, nothing pro-hibited a circus from taking acts that had been developed privately, usually by families of circus performers.

The gym was quieted by a pair of ballet teachers who had been around the school for years. Random rehearsals were stopped, but the hum of voices and clanking equipment continued. In the corner where he couldn't see, the pianist practiced while the first act set up.

The performers were all young, all good. The first was a trio of ladder balancers, two women and one man. The man was powerful, teeth showing in a confident grin. The women were slim, smiling, an interesting contrast: one dark, one light. The piano clanked a British rock song, badly played but recognizable. The act was excellent but a bit automatic, mechanical, lacking flair.

The second act performed to something by Mozart, which the pianist played a bit better. The performer was also better, a unicyclist with a round steel cage that he controlled, rolling it by riding his unicycle inside it. He looked a bit like a hamster in a plastic bubble, but he played clever variations on movement, near-disasters, and speed riding.

The third act was a slack-wire clown, excellent but too reminiscent of the early Popov routine.

It would take time, a year perhaps, to get to whichever act was selected. Perhaps he would never get to the performer and would have to go the route of dealing with one of the old acts. All of the old acts, however, would be dangerous prospects.

It wasn't as easy to corrupt circus performers as it would have been with some other professionals. Circus performers had prestige, good living conditions, a guaranteed lifetime of work. It would be a challenge, but as he stood in the shadows he looked for the signs of weakness in the faces of the young people below, the signs that had probably been in his own face when he had been down there. How quickly did the stage smile drop when the act was finished? Did the performer hurry the hug of approval from other students and back away? Was there a touch of uncertainty and a masked lack of confidence in the stride?

He looked for these things and saw his greatest hope in

the slack-wire clown. It would be hard to influence the decision, perhaps impossible, but the clown had the most promise for corruption. Yes, there was a future, a way out, with but one loose end: Katya Rashkovskaya, a most dangerous loose end. He went back to the first floor and found the office of a teacher who had once been in the New Circus. The teacher had a known drinking problem and debts. He could use money and Dimitri Mazaraki had plenty of money. He paused and examined himself in the glass of the office door, adjusted his mustache, patted down his hair, and stepped through the door.

Yuri Pon had not brought his knife. He was not planning to execute a prostitute on impulse. He had made that mistake once, on the subway, and had regretted it. Everything had gone wrong that time. The prostitute had worn a uniform and had turned out not to be a prostitute at all. He had worked too quickly. He had even been seen. No, he had to be careful, precise. He knew how deeply his emotions ran, and for that reason he forced himself to be cautious and methodical.

He would identify a prostitute, be absolutely sure that he was correct, follow her, and, if possible, observe her in the act. He would find out where she normally went, prepare himself, and, on the night chosen, execute her.

He took the metro to the Mayakovsky Station and made his way to the Byelorussian Railway Station, where he was sure to find what he was looking for if he were a bit patient. It didn't take long. He bought a coffee from an old woman at a stand in the station, sat with a copy of *Izvestia* in his hand, adjusted his glasses, and pretended to be waiting for a train. Occasionally, he would look up at the posted schedules to suggest to anyone who might be watching him that he had legitimate business.

In the course of the next two hours he saw three prostitutes attempting to pick up travelers coming in. He rejected two of the prostitutes immediately. They were not pretty enough. A third was a distinct possibility. She was blond, about twenty-five, and wearing a gray dress and a white top. She looked healthy, confident, not defiant. And she was not afraid to approach an occasional soldier. The fourth soldier she approached picked her up, and the two of them walked toward the massive front entrance of the station. Yuri gulped down his coffee, tucked his newspaper under his arm, and got up to follow them. He arrived at the entrance a step before they did and even held the door open for the couple to walk out. It was then that he got his first clear look at the woman. She was pretty but she was flawed. A dark purple birthmark about the size of a baby's hand ran from below her right ear down her neck. It didn't touch her face but it was there. He imagined the soldier kissing her in the dark, kissing her neck.

Yuri Pon did not follow them. He felt ill. His stomach was sour and the acid taste snaked into his mouth. The evening was hot and he had had a hard day. Nikolai would probably have passed out by now, so it would be safe to go back to the apartment. Tomorrow or the next night Yuri would try again. It would be hard to wait. He would try someplace else. He would be patient, careful, efficient. He would control his emotions. He would make his contribution. Tomorrow or the next night.

When Rostnikov walked down Krasikov Street toward his apartment that evening, he had a plan for the night. First, he would engage in small talk with Sarah. Before they ate, he would spend his forty minutes lifting weights in the corner of the room and she would read or watch television. During dinner he would suggest that they go for a walk and Sarah would accept. She would also know that he had something serious to say. On the walk he would tell her about Josef's posting to Afghanistan, try to comfort her, and hope she would have some words of comfort for him. They would stop for something, maybe an ice cream, and come home early to talk or read. It would, he thought, be a slow, perhaps sad, night in which he would not think of the KGB, of the Gray Wolfhound, of the man who had dived off Gogol's statue. He hoped it would not be one of those nights when bad news angered her, turned her against him, transformed him into the evil cossack of her imagination. These outbursts were always brief and regretted, but they lingered in his memory and he feared that frequent setbacks would increase the periods of anger. Her anger made him feel helpless. Rostnikov could deal with murderers, pompous superiors, scheming KGB officers. He could play their games, even gain a satisfaction from small triumphs, but his wife's emotion swept him away. He never considered joining her in anger. Rostnikov had learned even as a boy not to be angry. It wasn't that he controlled his anger. It was simply that he didn't feel it. The world was strange, sad, ironic, comic, even terrible, and, yes, there were people who were monsters. It wasn't that he forgave them. He often thought that anger might be far more satisfying than the frequent state of amused melancholy with which he felt most comfortable.

When he reached the apartment and stepped in, Porfiry Petrovich saw and accepted that the night he had planned was not to be. At the wooden table that had been given them by Sarah's mother sat his wife and two men. Sarah, her red hair tied loosely back, looked up at him with a small smile. Rostnikov moved to her and kissed her moist forehead. The warm evening brought out her distinct, natural smell, which always came back to him as a nearly forgotten pleasant memory.

He shook hands with Sasha Tkach and then reached out with both hands to shake the left hand of Emil Karpo. Karpo's grip was firm.

"The hand is strong," said Rostnikov, sitting at the last unoccupied chair and reaching for the bread in the center of the table. Tkach had a teacup in front of him.

"It is better than it was yesterday, and yesterday it was better than the day before," Karpo said.

"Cousin Alex is a good doctor," said Sarah with pride.

"He's a good doctor," Karpo agreed.

Rostnikov looked at his two unexpected guests, who looked at each other to determine who would speak first. When Porfiry Petrovich was chief inspector in the Procurator's Office, the three of them had been an unofficial team.

Rostnikov had used their strengths, worked around their weaknesses, encouraged their initiative. In turn, they had given him loyalty. It was not the first night they had sat around this table, and Rostnikov hoped that it would not be the last. From his pocket, Rostnikov removed the pistol he had taken from Katya Rashkovskaya and placed it carefully on the table.

"It is no longer loaded," Rostnikov said, turning to Sarah.

"Did someone . . . ?" she began.

"Just to shoot a toilet," said Rostnikov.

"A TK," Karpo said quietly, looking at the weapon. "A six-point-three-five-millimeter blowback automatic of good quality. The pistol was supposedly designed by a man named Korovine in 1930. There is a mystery about Korovine. He designed weapons in Belgium during the First World War and took out a patent for a double-action internal-hammer lock for automatic pistols, though there seems to be no evidence that it was ever actually manufactured. Then, after disappearing for almost ten years, he designed the TK in the Soviet Union and was never heard of or from again."

"So you can tell me nothing about this weapon?" Rostnikov asked with a smile.

"On the contrary, Comrade Inspector," said Karpo. "It is striker fired and . . . You are making a joke of some kind?"

"A poor one, Emil," said Rostnikov with a sigh, looking at Tkach, who stared into his empty teacup.

Rostnikov caught his wife's eye and nodded at Tkach.

"More tea, Sasha?" Sarah asked, getting up.

"A little," he said, pushing back the wisp of hair that fell over his eyes.

"Sasha was saying that the baby is outgrowing her clothes," Sarah said, moving to the teakettle on the stove in the kitchen. "She'll be ready for the suit I knitted for her when the first cold days come."

Rostnikov removed the pistol from the table, placed it back in his pocket, chewed on his bread, and waited. Sarah came back with a cup of tea for him and poured more for Tkach, who thanked her.

"Today I went to the circus, the New Circus," Rostnikov said after swallowing a mouthful of bread.

"I was near there this morning, near the university," Tkach said. He seemed about to add something but stopped.

"All right," Rostnikov said with a sigh. "Emil, you begin."

Karpo looked at Sarah and then at Sasha before fixing his eyes on Rostnikov and saying, "You were principal investigator on the murder of Sonia Melyodska, a soldier, in the Vdnkh Metro Station last year. You filed a report."

"In November, the third week," Rostnikov said, reaching for another piece of bread.

"Precisely," Karpo agreed.

"And?"

"And why did you file the report with those of the serial killer of prostitutes?" Karpo asked.

The normal question at this point might have been Why do you want to know? or What's going on? But Rostnikov had learned to be patient with Emil Karpo, whose own patience was infinite and whose sense of humor was nonexistent.

"I did not file it with the reports on the serial killer of prostitutes," Rostnikov said. "It never entered my head that there could be a connection. I investigated for two weeks, relatives and friends of the murdered woman, the possibility of a random killing by a subway thief. I worked with Zelach searching for witnesses. Nothing. I submitted the report to open file."

"I found it in the file of murdered prostitutes," Karpo said.

Rostnikov was well aware that the prostitute killer was not Karpo's responsibility. It might be reasonable to ask why he was even reading the file. Rostnikov didn't ask. Instead he looked at Sasha Tkach, who didn't appear to be listening.

"Sasha," Rostnikov said, rubbing the stubble on his own

chin. "How would you account for this puzzle?"

"I, I wasn't . . ." Tkach stammered as if awakened from sleep.

"You should," Rostnikov said.

Sarah asked if the two guests were staying for dinner. Both said they were not. She excused herself and began working in the kitchen while the three men continued.

"Emil has found a report on a murder I investigated in the wrong file," Rostnikov explained.

"A misfiling." Tkach shrugged. "Someone pulled your report and accidentally placed it in the wrong file. It happens."

"The number on Inspector Rostnikov's report is in the three hundred series. The number of the serial killing file is in the two hundred series. They are not close," said Karpo. "In addition, the original number on Inspector Rostnikov's report has been lined out and the new number written neatly in its place. There are no initials to indicate who did this or why."

"So?" asked Tkach, looking at Rostnikov.

"Someone must think my killer and the serial killer are the same," said Rostnikov. "But who thinks so and why? Why would anyone besides me even pull the report? Why would they refile it without talking to me and to the investigator in charge of the serial murders? I gather that—"

"I called Inspector Ivanov," said Karpo. "No one spoke to him about the report. He did not make the change. He suggested that I simply pull it out and return the report to the proper file."

"No doubt he also wanted to know why you were reading the file of a case assigned to him," Rostnikov said.

"I told him it seemed to be tied in to a case on which I was working," said Karpo.

"Well, Sasha?" asked Rostnikov, reaching for the last of the bread. The smell of boiling *rassolnik rybny*, noodle soup, had reminded Rostnikov of his hunger.

"A joke?"

"The risks associated with such a joke make that unlikely," said Karpo, who had obviously thought about this possibility.

"A lunatic in the file room?" Tkach tried again. "Sabotage? The KGB? A test?"

"All possible," said Rostnikov. "But there is another possibility."

"I don't see it," sighed Tkach.

"That there is a person, possibly an officer, who has access to the files and knows something but is unwilling or unable to come forward and say it. Perhaps he knows of KGB involvement in the murders, or that a prominent figure or the relative of a prominent figure, possibly even a member of the Politburo, is involved in the murders. It has happened before. This officer is suggesting that someone else pick up the pieces."

"There is another possibility," said Karpo.

"That the murderer is a police officer who wanted the reports of his killings kept together," said Tkach.

Rostnikov smiled in appreciation and reached over to pat the younger man's back.

"Stay for soup," he said. "Sarah, is there enough soup?"

"Enough for all. More than you and I can eat," she called back.

Tkach nodded and Karpo said nothing for an instant and then nodded his agreement. Rostnikov got up and moved into the kitchen to get another loaf of bread. Sarah looked at him as she cut a cucumber.

"Don't look like that, Porfiry Petrovich," she said quietly.

"Look? Look like what?" he answered, reaching over her for the day-old black bread in the cupboard.

"We'll talk about it later," she whispered.

"Talk about?"

"Josef," she said. She cut the cucumber into smaller pieces, turning her head from him. "I got a call at the shop today to tell me that he had been, had been transferred to Afghanistan. They said they had already told you."

"That was kind of them," Rostnikov said, putting his arm around her shoulder.

"No, it wasn't," she said, holding back the tears.

"No, it wasn't," he agreed. "It was a warning to me, to us."

She said nothing.

"We'll talk later," he said and returned to the other room to pass the bread around and pour fresh tea.

For the next half hour they worked out a plan to deal with Karpo's case. Only after they had finished their dinner did Rostnikov turn to Tkach.

"This morning I located, and obtained evidence against, two black marketers dealing in video recorders and video-tapes," he said. "I turned my report in to Deputy Procurator Khabolov, who said that he would personally investigate. I believe he may plan to profit by and from these black marketers."

"And this surprises you?" Rostnikov said, looking at Karpo, whose thin lips were even more pale and tight than usual. Corruption was accepted by most Soviet citizens, but to Emil Karpo every act of corruption was an attack on the system to which he had dedicated his life. Corruption by a member of the police was especially painful. Karpo's impulse, Rostnikov was sure, was to confront and punish, to punish severely.

"No," sighed Tkach. "I'm afraid that I will be used to cover for whatever he plans to do, that I will be blamed if he is found out."

"A reasonable conclusion, from what we know of Deputy Khabolov," said Rostnikov. "And you'd like some help in protecting yourself?"

"Yes," said Tkach.

"And the black marketers?" asked Rostnikov.

Tkach shrugged.

"One of them has a daughter, a young girl," Tkach said softly. "She's about nine or ten."

Rostnikov looked at Karpo, who betrayed his feelings only by meeting the inspector's eyes.

"Emil Karpo thinks that the existence of the child is not relevant, that we do not excuse corruption for any cause, that the child might well be better off as a ward of the state. Am I right, Emil?"

"You are right, Comrade," Karpo said.

"I don't know," said Tkach.

"Well," said Rostnikov, standing to ease the strain on his leg, "let's see what we can work out."

At precisely eleven o'clock that night, Osip and Felix Gorgasali sat in their trailer, the blackened curtains down, and talked quietly so they would not wake Osip's wife and daughter. They talked about, wondered about, feared, what they would have to face the next morning. A uniformed policeman had arrived late in the evening at the trailer to inform them that they were to be in the office of Deputy Procurator Khabolov at exactly eight the next morning. The policeman had given no explanation, and they had been too stunned to ask for one.

From time to time, Felix muttered *nichevo*, the Russian word for "nothing," which conveyed resignation, stoicism, the idea that whatever might be the problem, you shouldn't let it get to you. Life is too full of explosions. One cannot allow oneself to be destroyed by fear of them.

"*Nichevo*," Osip agreed, wondering which shirt to wear the next morning, knowing that he wouldn't be able to sleep.

At precisely eleven o'clock that night, Sasha Tkach rubbed his wife's back as they lay in bed. They didn't speak. Maya loved to have her back rubbed, and let out a soft, appreciative purr as he moved his hands up from her spine to her shoulders.

The book of fairy tales was propped against the table near the baby's bed. Pulcharia turned and gurgled in harmony with her mother's hum, and Sasha smiled in the darkness, forgetting his anxiety.

At precisely eleven o'clock that night, Yuri Pon considered smashing a chair over Nikolai's head. Nikolai, the filthy dwarf, was snoring, snoring as he never had before.

Yuri went to Nikolai's bed and prodded him. The sleeping man snorted, spewed forth an alcoholic belch, turned on his side, and snored much more quietly. Nikolai had not changed clothes, had not shaved, had simply taken off his shirt and shoes and fallen asleep.

The prodding by Yuri would be effective for about ten minutes while Nikolai approached wakefulness and then gradually retreated to the depth of whatever dreams he had, dreams that quickened his heartbeat and made him snore like a wounded cat.

Yuri wanted to sleep, had to sleep. He had to get up early for work. There was so much to do. But going to sleep with this snoring and the feeling of incompleteness was impossible. It was as if Yuri were hungry, but he had eaten ravenously when he got home that night, had eaten and eaten as he had as a boy, a fat boy. The eating left him still hungry, but hunger wasn't quite what he now felt. Unfulfilled. That was it. There was only one thing that would make that feeling, that near-pain, go away. He would have to do more work for the state, for the people, for Russia. He would have to find a prostitute soon. He would have to find her and kill her. If he lived long enough, he might have to find and kill every prostitute in Moscow inside the Outer Ring Road. There might be hundreds. They might be replaced by others. He might be caught. That would be the worst of all, to be caught and sent to jail knowing that they were still out there. It would be like forever living suspended over a jigsaw puzzle with one piece left to put in and never being able to place the piece where it belonged. As he lay in the darkness of the room, he imagined himself standing over a table with a jigsaw puzzle laid out before him. He couldn't see the puzzle but he knew he held the final piece in his hand. He couldn't quite see the piece, either, but he knew it was heavy, too heavy to keep holding. He also knew that he could not put it down, and he struggled to stay awake, not fall into this dream, a dream he had created. His eyes wouldn't open. In his near-dream he looked down at the puzzle and suddenly knew the puzzle was very important.

It was more than just a thing to pass the time. The solution to the puzzle would be the solution to something about himself.

He forced himself to look, forced himself to pull the image that lay flat and unfinished before him into perspective. It was a woman, the head and shoulders of a woman, but he could not make the image hold still, become sharp, and the piece in his hand made his muscles ache with pain. He turned his eyes to his hand. He turned slowly in fear and saw that his upraised right hand clutched a human eye, a pulsating human eye with a nerve dangling between his fingers like a red worm. Yuri wanted to scream, drop the eye, but he knew he couldn't. The eye in his hand looked down at the puzzle, and Yuri followed its gaze and saw that the woman in the puzzle was missing an eye. For an instant, less than the time it would take to be sure, he thought the woman in the puzzle was his mother and then it was a woman he sometimes saw at the grocer's and then it was no one he knew and then it was the face of the uniformed woman he had killed in the subway, the one on the stairs, the one who had said something to him, called him a name, when he accidentally bumped into her. He had seen that she was nothing but a prostitute in a uniform. Even if she were really in the army, she would be a prostitute when she got out, as she had surely been before she went in. She had called him a name, had called him a perverted fat pig. After all he had done, all he planned to do. He who was always so careful, so neat. She had called him a pig and he had lost control, had pulled out his pocket knife, had shown her what a pig could do. And now he stood holding her eye. Had he cut out her eye? He didn't remember. He didn't think so. He couldn't remember the report. Perhaps he could check it in the morning. He didn't want the eye that squirmed in his hand, squirmed wet like petroleum jelly as his arm turned to stone. Yes, he would return the eye. Oh, please, let him return the eye, he begged whatever gods might be, begged his hand, but neither the gods nor his body answered.

* * *

At eleven o'clock that evening, Emil Karpo finished his arm exercises, clenched his teeth to keep from making a sound, and felt the thin drops of perspiration on his forehead. He wiped the moisture away with his sleeve and moved to his desk, where he had laid out three pages of names. After his meeting with Rostnikov, Karpo had returned to Petrovka, gone to the records room, and told the night clerk that he needed a copy of the complete list of those who had access to the files, who were authorized to go beyond the desk.

If the clerk had any thoughts of withholding the list from the gaunt specter before him, he did not voice or show them. He dutifully supplied a copy of the current authorization list and hoped that Karpo would take it and leave. Instead of leaving, the Vampire had asked the clerk a series of strange questions about how long he had been night clerk, where he had been at certain times of the year, and where he lived. The inspector was obviously mad, as quite a few investigators seemed to be, and the best thing to do was humor him. The clerk answered the questions, and Karpo left without explanation.

And now Karpo stood over his desk looking down at the list of eighty-six names including inspector-level personnel in the MVD and the Procurator's Office plus clerical personnel. At least fifteen on the list were KGB, though they were not identified as such. They would be the most difficult to check out, but it could be done. Some of the checking could be done without the knowledge of the individual. Work schedules might well clear a good number by showing that they were in a specific place or ill or accounted for at the time of any of the murders. It would not be easy and might take a great deal of time, but the expenditure of time did not bother Emil Karpo. He would methodically go through the list and check them all. Then he might have to check them again. In the end, it might turn out to be none of them, in which case he would have to find another way to deal with the killer. It was just a matter of time and of his ability to make his mind and body continue to function.

He sat at his desk and ordered his healing left arm to move, and it moved to pick up the pen.

At eleven o'clock that night, Dimitri Mazaraki stood alone in the near-darkness of the ring of the New Circus. The night lights cast shadows that merged with the darkness. Beneath his feet, Mazaraki felt the hardness of the concrete floor—below which was the ice level, which could be raised in a few minutes—and below that the water pool, which could be brought forth almost instantly. Layers below layers below layers. Nothing quite what it seemed, just as the circus wasn't quite what it seemed.

Mazaraki liked standing alone looking out at the empty seats and the further darkness, where he knew the empty seats continued. The night sounds didn't frighten him: the creaking, the warping. He felt powerful knowing he was impressive and tall, his mustache fine. He resisted the impulse to put his hands on his hips, but he didn't resist the urge to grin. He would sleep in his office this night. He had done it before. He would sleep in his office and wake up to finish the plans for the next circus tour, which he was to have ready when the director returned. He would suggest the acts at the circus school he thought might replace the Pesknoko troupe. He would praise the slack-wire clown. Dimitri Mazaraki could be patient about most things, but there were things that did not allow one to exercise patience. One of those things was Katya Rashkovskaya. He decided that she would have to be killed very, very soon.

At eleven o'clock that night, after Sarah had gone to sleep in the bedroom, Porfiry Petrovich sat in his underwear in the living room of their two-room apartment and read the end of his current 87th Precinct novel. He had read it too quickly, had failed to savor it as he always promised himself to do. He would make up for it by reading the book again, though he wasn't sure he liked the grisly ending with the Calypso woman . . . No, he wasn't sure he liked it, though he had enjoyed being with Meyer and Carella and Kling and the others. As he put down the book it reminded him that he had met someone that day who had looked like one of the Isola policemen. Yes, the assistant at the New Circus who had a white streak in his hair like Hawes. That memory triggered another, and Rostnikov got up to return his book to the shelf in the corner and remove two plumbing books to bring to Katya Rashkovskaya. To get to the books, Rostnikov had to move his small trophy, the bronze trophy he had won in the Moscow Senior Weightlifting Championships three years ago.

Each night, as he had done an hour ago this night, Rostnikov had rolled out his mat, removed his weights and bars from the lower shelf, and put on his sweatshirt to work out within a few feet of the trophy. Tonight he had worked out far later than he had in years. With no carpet on the floor he knew that he was making considerable noise for the Barkans in the apartment below, even though he was as quiet as he could be. The Barkans would not complain, not because they were so understanding, but because Rostnikov was a policeman and it did not pay for citizens to complain about the police. Nonetheless, Rostnikov tried to work out early whenever possible. The workout was essential. He could lose himself in the weights as he could in nothing else, and each day for almost an hour it was necessary to engage in that meditation with weights. Tonight had been no different in spite of the long talk with Sarah.

They had walked for an hour and talked in the park after Karpo and Tkach left. They had talked of Josef, reassured each other about the news from Afghanistan, remembered that Josef had only four months left of his army service. They did not talk about leaving the Soviet Union. Sarah had realized and finally accepted that there was nothing to be done that could get them out, that her husband had risked his career and possibly their lives to try to get exit visas and had failed. She accepted. Even Josef's new assignment she accepted with pain and fear, but she accepted. Rostnikov had put an arm around her and hugged her awkwardly in the park, and she had allowed herself to cry—but just for an instant. And then they had returned to the apartment.

After he had put the plumbing books by the front door, Rostnikov turned out the light and made his way to the bedroom, where he got into bed as quietly as he could without waking Sarah. Rostnikov had to be up early for the dreaded morning meeting with the Gray Wolfhound. He hoped he could avoid any new assignment of substance. He wanted to return to the circus. The memory of the smell of the circus came to him suddenly, elusively, like the scent of some flower or candy or young girl smelled once in childhood. And as he went to sleep he knew, as certainly as he knew that smell, that Katya Rashkovskaya would have to tell him the secret she guarded or her life might be as brief as that remembered scent.

FIVE

AT PRECISELY SEVEN O'CLOCK THE NEXT MORNING, A Tuesday, Emil Karpo did not bother to knock at the door on the second level below ground in the Petrovka Police Station. He turned the handle and pushed the door open with his right hand and was greeted by a metallic whirring sound like the drill of a dentist. Karpo, his left hand holding a frayed, black leather briefcase filled with the neatly written notes he had spent the night writing, stepped in and closed the door.

The room looked more like a way station to the garbage dump than a laboratory. Its clutter irritated Karpo, to whom symmetry, reason, and order were essential. But this was Paulinin's lab, and Paulinin was an enigma to the policeman.

Karpo stepped past a headless dressmaker's bust of a portly woman, avoided a cardboard box full of bottles on the floor, squeezed by a table piled high with books and metal pieces that looked as if they came from inside some mechanical children's toy.

A man in a blue smock with his back to the door leaned over a table in the corner of the windowless room. The man's hands rose delicately, as if he were engaged in a surgical operation or were conducting a particularly difficult piece by Stravinsky.

"I'm busy, Inspector," Paulinin cried over the whirring sound with a wave of his hand, his back still turned.

Karpo took a step closer and stood patiently, silently, in front of Paulinin's desk, the top of which was covered by books and the miscellany of past investigations. The set of teeth that had been on the desk the last time Karpo had visited the laboratory was still there, grinning atop a small abacus stained with dried blood.

"Inspector Karpo," Paulinin sighed, his back still turned. "I'm...ah, ha. There." The whirring sound stopped.

With a triumphant look on his face, Paulinin, a bespectacled, nearsighted monkey with an oversized head topped by wild gray-black hair, turned to face his visitor for the first time. In his hand he held something that looked to Karpo like a human heart. Behind Paulinin, on the table, was a metal tray filled with blood and a small white machine with a glass bowl attached to it.

"A centrifuge didn't work," Paulinin said, looking around for someplace to put the organ in his hand. "A three-hundred-ruble centrifuge."

His glasses were in danger of falling off the end of his nose, but Paulinin had no free hand with which to adjust them. He tried to push the glasses back with his shoulder and failed.

"And do you know what worked?" he asked, balancing the heart in one hand and grabbing a plastic bucket from the floor.

"No," said Karpo.

"That," Paulinin said in triumph, nodding back at the metal-and-glass object on the laboratory table. The plastic bucket contained something that looked like coffee grounds. Paulinin dumped them into the metal tray on the table and just managed to drop the heart into the now-empty plastic bucket.

"Paulinin—" Karpo began, but the scientist held up a

hand to stop him as he pushed his glasses back on his nose, which brought a smile to his simian face and a streak of blood to his forehead.

"Do you know what that is?" he asked Karpo, glancing at him and then moving to the small sink in the corner of the room. "Huh?"

"No," said Karpo patiently.

Paulinin pushed some rubber tubes and a glass beaker out of the way and turned on the water. As he washed, he looked back at Karpo and said, "A food processor. The French and Americans use them for chopping food into pieces so small that they turn to paste almost. You can put anything except solid mineral products in it. Well, almost anything."

He turned off the water and faced Karpo as he dried his hands on his smock.

"I got it from a KGB man named . . . a KGB man I've done some things for," Paulinin whispered, though his laboratory was almost certainly not wired and the door was soundproof.

"Interesting," said Karpo at near-attention, waiting.

"They were through with this heart," Paulinin said, biting his lower lip and looking down at the plastic bucket affectionately. "Through with it. Case closed. Autopsy finished. X ray failed to show anything. Natural death. They gave me the heart. And do you know what I found in that heart? Do you know what that French food processor and I found in that heart?"

"I do not know, Comrade," said Karpo.

"Gold, gold, gold. Tiny fragments of gold," Paulinin said with a smile on his bloody face as he absently reached up to push down his hair. "Someone injected gold into his bloodstream. It blocked his vessels. A man with a heart condition. Gold. Can you imagine?"

"I—" Karpo began.

"And you want to know what I'm going to do with this information?" Paulinin asked, moving behind his desk and clapping his hands together as he sat.

"No," said Karpo.

"Nothing," said Paulinin, blowing out air. "I think our political people may know something about this. The old Cheka eliminated two politicals in a similar manner for symbolic reasons in 1930. And then various murders have been committed involving the introduction of small particles of metal orally or through an orifice. One particularly interesting case in Syria last year involved the introduction of a catheter into . . . But I sense a certain disinterest in you, Comrade Emil. So, if the KGB finds out I have the heart, they may ask why and wonder what I found. I will tell them I used it for experiments on tissue, that I discovered nothing, that I chopped the pieces up and flushed them, which is what I will do. I don't want certain people with a strained sense of humor to inject gold into my urinary system so that some morning I would wake up pissing away hundreds of rubles in gold."

Paulinin looked up at Karpo expectantly.

"I made a joke, Comrade Inspector," Paulinin said.

"I know," replied Karpo.

"Why do I like you, Inspector?"

"I had no idea you did," said Karpo.

"I really did find gold in that heart," said Paulinin softly, turning to look at the food processor. "Now I've sifted it and have enough gold to pay for a second food processor. Why would anyone kill with gold?"

"I don't know," said Karpo.

"Aren't you curious?" asked Paulinin, starting to get up, looking over at the bucket, and sitting down again.

"No," said Karpo.

"What do you want?" Paulinin asked.

Karpo opened the battered briefcase and removed the stack of papers held together by a large spring clip. He found a place on the desk atop a book in a foreign language and placed the stack on it.

"You have a work process report?" Paulinin said, adjusting his glasses and reaching for the papers.

"No," said Karpo.

"And no 3245 approval?"

"No," said Karpo. "The case is not officially mine. Just

as the death of the former possessor of that heart is not officially your responsibility."

"Unlike you, I am always curious," said Paulinin. "I am not always temperate, either, or, as you know, I would have more space, more equipment, more responsibility. But am I bitter?"

"Yes," said Karpo.

"A little, perhaps," Paulinin agreed. "What do you want?"

"I have the names of a number of people on these lists with some information about each of them," Karpo explained. "Each person should be in the central computer file with more data. I cannot have access to the computer without a case report. In addition, I do not know how to program for the answers I need."

"And you want me to . . . ?" Paulinin began, reaching up to touch his bloody forehead. He brought his hand down and looked a bit puzzled by the sight of blood on his just-washed hands.

"Put these names into the computer. Ask the questions I tell you to ask. I want to narrow this list down."

Paulinin picked up the clipped papers and began to flip through them.

"I recognize these names, most of these names," said Paulinin, almost to himself. Then he put the pile down and looked at the set of false teeth. With a fresh sigh, he moved the teeth and picked up the abacus. "How many names?"

"I've got it down to forty-one," said Karpo. "Do you want to know why I want this done?"

"No," said Paulinin. "What I don't know, I can't tell later. This eccentricity of mine offers protection only as long as I prove to be a creative source of information. You understand?"

"Perfectly," said Karpo.

"You need this—"

"Immediately," said Karpo.

"How many questions do you have about each of these?"

"Five," said Karpo.

"Five," said Paulinin, who glanced at the first sheet of the pile of papers Karpo had given him and began to make some calculations on the abacus. The beads clicked quickly under his fingers for a few seconds and then he looked up. "Maybe an hour. Maybe two. You want something to eat, drink, while you wait?"

"No," said Karpo.

"Then," said Paulinin, putting down the abacus and rising, "let's narrow your list."

As Paulinin sat at the computer terminal in his laboratory and Karpo watched over his shoulder, nine floors above them the morning meeting of Colonel Snitkonoy's staff was about to end.

The Gray Wolfhound had listened with a knowing shake of his head to Pankov's and Major Grigorovich's reports. Something about the Wolfhound's manner alerted Rostnikov. Snitkonoy was not listening to the reports. That was clear from his knowing nods, the inappropriateness of the moments at which he decided to grunt or smile with approval. His uniform neatly pressed, his hair very recently cut, Snitkonoy was putting on his act. Pankov sweated and didn't seem in the least aware that the Wolfhound had another prey in mind. Grigorovich noticed. He relaxed his back slightly after he began his report because he quickly knew that he, too, was not the focus of the Wolfhound's real attention.

Not once had Snitkonoy mentioned his visit the day before to the factory. Not once did he say anything about his influence, his busy schedule. What was even more disturbing was that he gave no words of wisdom to the trio that sat as he paced. In addition, he had made no lists and drawn no diagrams on the blackboard.

"Inspector Rostnikov," the Wolfhound said in his deep voice that had been known to carry throughout Dynamo Stadium without benefit of a microphone. "You have several concurrent investigations."

"Yes, Comrade," Rostnikov agreed, alert, anticipating but keeping his voice low and a bit lazy. "The gang of youths defacing transportation centers, the pickpocket, metro stations with paint seem to be—"

"The *tsirk*," Snitkonoy said, suddenly leaning forward over the table, his medals jangling on his chest. "What is going on with the circus business, the accident?"

"I made some preliminary inquiries—"

"And found what you believe to be a connection between the fall of the man in Gogol Square and the aerialist?" the Wolfhound said, leaning even further forward toward Rostnikov. Grigorovich, who sat between the two men, was ramrod straight and still.

"Possibly, Comrade, possibly," agreed Rostnikov.

"And you took an officer on standard patrol and assigned him to protect a woman from the circus?" said Snitkonoy with a smile directed at Pankov, who shrank back and smiled in return.

"The woman was distraught and, possibly, a potential victim of the person who may have killed or induced the deaths of the two circus performers," said Rostnikov.

"They were accidents," said Snitkonoy, standing up and clasping his hands behind his back in the familiar pose of his frequent photographs.

"Possibly," said Rostnikov with a shrug as he watched the colonel begin to pace.

"You will remove the officer from that assignment and you will cease this investigation," said the colonel, pacing but not looking at Rostnikov.

"As you say, Colonel," Rostnikov said, looking down at his pad and fighting the urge to fill in a quick caricature of the prancing fool. The urge was followed by a weaker but distinct urge to grab the colonel, lift him up, and shake him like a toy till his brains were rearranged in a more functional manner or ceased to work altogether.

"You have done it again, Inspector Rostnikov," the Wolfhound said with a shake of his head. "Once again. You have blundered into something that . . . doesn't concern you. Do you understand?"

"The KGB has an interest in the case." Rostnikov sighed, put down his pencil, and sat back.

"I was unaware of the interest of another investigative branch when I approved the assignment," said the Wolfhound. "This morning I was fully briefed on the situation. You are to drop the investigation."

Which meant that Snitkonoy knew nothing, had been told nothing other than that he should have Rostnikov back away from whatever he was doing. It meant that the case, which had been deemed to have some importance, was far beyond the petty nonsense the Gray Wolfhound was allowed to handle. It wasn't at all unusual for the KGB to pick up a case once preliminary investigative reports had been filed and decide that the situation was political or economic.

It was also clear to Rostnikov that the Wolfhound had probably been treated with no great respect by whoever had ordered him to pass the word on to Rostnikov.

"Find the metro painters, Comrade Inspector," the Wolfhound said, turning his back to the seated trio. "Find the pickpocket."

"Yes, Comrade Colonel," Rostnikov said, putting his hands below the table so that the others would not see his fists tighten, his knuckles go white.

"That is all, gentlemen," the Wolfhound said with a dismissing wave of his right hand, his back still to them. Pankov gathered his papers and was out of the meeting room almost instantly. Major Grigorovich moved deliberately and just slowly enough so that Rostnikov might not think that he was hurrying away to escape the wrath of the Wolfhound. Rostnikov took a deep, silent breath, stood up, gathered his notes, and limped toward the door. As he touched the handle, the deep voice behind him said, "Rostnikov."

Rostnikov turned to the colonel, whose back was still to him. The tightly gripped fingers of Snitkonoy's hands, clasped behind his back, were as white as Rostnikov's had been under the table.

"You were in the war, weren't you, Inspector? That's how you got your limp."

"Yes," said Rostnikov, wondering where they were going now.

"I was one of the youngest field officers in the Great War," said the Wolfhound, turning to face Rostnikov. There was a look on the older man's face Rostnikov had never seen before.

"Younger people who have no experience with combat, have never faced death, now tell those of us who know something of what it means how we should react to it," Snitkonoy said. "Do you understand what I am saying here, Comrade Inspector?"

The Wolfhound was clearly apologizing for his behavior during the meeting, which made Rostnikov wonder if Snitkonoy were quite the fool he thought him to be. Most likely he was a fool whose massive ego had been pierced by a young KGB agent who had no time for or interest in the egos of old men.

"I understand, Colonel," Rostnikov said.

"Good," said Snitkonoy with a deep sigh, raising his head and his voice. "Good."

There was nothing more to say. Rostnikov left the room, picked up the plumbing books from the drawer in his desk in which he had put them, and headed for Lenin Prospekt and the apartment of Katya Rashkovskaya.

As Porfiry Petrovich Rostnikov left the meeting room, two floors below him Felix and Osip Gorgasali sat on a wooden bench outside the office of Deputy Procurator Khabolov. They had been waiting for almost two hours while others came and went. They had been escorted up the elevator and to the bench by a uniformed MVD officer who said nothing to them, did not even look at them. He had simply pointed at the bench in the dark hallway, and they knew that they were to sit.

Osip had suggested that they dress shabbily, two lowly merchants just able to make ends meet. Felix, being older, prevailed, however, and they had worn respectable suits with ties, though the clothing was not new. In fact, both men had complete wardrobes of imported Polish clothes and even some American clothing. Osip owned two pairs of American Wrangler jeans.

They said almost nothing as they sat. From time to time the dark and hairy Osip played with a shaving cut on his chin. He was afraid of bleeding in front of the deputy procurator, but he couldn't keep his fingers from his face. Each time the office door in front of them opened, Osip jumped slightly and let out a small groan. Both men needed a toilet. Neither would rise or ask.

And then, at a little before ten, a burly man in a shaggy suit stepped out of the deputy procurator's office and motioned to the brothers Gorgasali to enter. The burly man stepped past them and walked down the hallway. Osip was reminded instantly of the moment in *The Wizard of Oz* when the scarecrow, the lion, and the tin woodsman walk with Dorothy into the lair of Oz. *The Wizard of Oz* was one of Natalya's favorite tapes. His daughter had seen it twenty or thirty times before Felix and Osip sold it to a *Pravda* editor for 250 rubles. Osip had, however, made a copy, which wasn't as good as the original but that—

"Sit," said the man behind the desk, breaking in on Osip's thoughts of the Emerald City.

The brothers sat on the two straight-backed wooden chairs facing the desk while the man behind it, his head down, continued to write on a pad of yellow paper. The man wrote for about five minutes, reread what he had written, gave the two men an icy look of appraisal, and then placed the yellow pad to the side of the desk.

"Do you know why you are here?" asked Khabolov.

"No, Comrade," said Felix. "We're just merchants, booksellers. We've witnessed no crime, committed no crime. We are honest citizens of the Soviet Union trying to make a living for—"

Khabolov's hand went up and Felix stopped. Osip was filled with a sudden fear that he would be asked to speak and would be unable to do so. He was the frightened lion.

"We know all about you," Khabolov said, looking over at his yellow pad. "I plan personally to inventory your entire collection of tapes and machines."

Osip couldn't help himself. A burst of fear let loose within him and released a loud sob. Felix looked at him angrily, but Osip could think only of prison, of his wife, daughter. Had he remained a simple bookseller, had he ignored this brother who had always ordered him around, gotten him into trouble, he would be breathing normally now—poor, but facing life.

Khabolov ignored the sobbing Gorgasali brother and looked at the older one with the white hair who might be pissing in his pants but was able to hold on to a facade of confused innocence. The two men before Khabolov were ripe. This same scene had worked well before, in Odessa with the typewriter thieves, and was working even better now.

"It was all my idea," Felix said, his shoulders dropping, at the same instant his sobbing brother pointed to him and burst out with, "It was all his idea."

With this, Felix instantly abandoned his ill-conceived moment of martyrdom, pointed at his brother, and shouted, "He lies. He threatened me to take responsibility. He beat me. It was his doing. I tried to get out but—"

"He tried," Osip said sarcastically, looking at Deputy Procurator Khabolov for support and getting none. "He forced my poor wife, my beautiful little daughter. Wait. I have a picture of my Natalya right here."

Desperately, Osip fumbled in his pocket and came out with his wallet while Felix said, "What does that prove? That proves nothing. He beats his wife and daughter."

"I . . . never. I love them both. Here, here," Osip cried, pushing his brother's restraining hand away and passing the wallet to the unsmiling man behind the desk.

Khabolov took the wallet, and Osip sat back with a small sense of frightened triumph.

"This is a very nice wallet. Canadian," said Khabolov.

"Canadian, yes," said Osip. "A gift to me from an old friend. I'd like to make it a gift to you for your kindness, your understanding."

Felix snorted in disgust and put his head down as Khabolov threw the wallet back to Osip.

"Are you attempting to bribe an officer of the state?" Khabolov said, fixing his eyes on Osip, who was now completely panicked, without any sense of response or direction. All he could do was shake his head no as he clutched the wallet to his stomach with both hands. Osip looked to his older brother for help, but Felix was looking at the floor, defeated.

"Comrades," Khabolov said, "I want you to do something."

Osip didn't hear the words. He simply sobbed and clutched his wallet, but Felix lifted his eyes at the words of the deputy procurator.

"Anything," said Felix.

"I want you to do some work for me in an investigation. I want the two of you to take part in a long-term government investigation of illegal marketing of videotapes and machines," said Khabolov, meeting Felix's eyes. There was an electric instant of understanding, and Felix sat up with new hope.

"We would be honored to help in any way we could serve the state, Comrade Procurator," Felix said over his brother's sobbing.

"Good," said Khabolov. "Your entire inventory will be taken over by the state. You will be permitted to continue to operate and keep a reasonable percentage of your profits. Let us say. . ."

"Seventy-five percent," said Felix, reaching over and digging his nails into his brother's calf to shut him up.

"Forty percent," said Khabolov.

"Forty percent," agreed Felix.

"You will report directly to me, deal directly with me," said Khabolov. "You will never return here again. All contact will be made through me or my son, Andreyev, who will take reports on all of your customers and all transactions. It will be necessary from time to time for us to confiscate certain pieces of equipment and tapes that Andreyev or I will select for investigatory purposes."

"Our inventory is small," said Felix with a sigh.

Osip had stopped sobbing and was beginning to realize

that the nature of the conversation had changed, that Felix was sounding like himself, that some kind of deal was being made.

"It will have to sustain itself if you and your brother are to remain a useful part of the undercover operation I am planning."

Which meant, Felix understood, that as long as he and Osip supplied the deputy procurator with all the free video equipment and tapes that he wanted and made him their senior partner they would remain free and in business. The price was high, but the alternative was prison, possibly even execution, and certainly poverty. Besides, the protection of the deputy procurator might be very comforting.

"We will do exactly as you say," said Felix.

"Exactly," echoed Osip as Felix reached over to tug at his brother's sleeve.

"Good," said Khabolov, with what may have been a slight smile. "Your patriotism will be rewarded. Perhaps there will even be a medal awarded at the end of this investigation, though, I must tell you, it looks as if the investigation may turn out to be a very long one."

"Whatever we must do to serve the state and the people will be done." Felix sighed.

Osip's sobs had departed, first replaced by a bland, open-mouthed incredulity and then by a slight, hopeful smile, as his eyes darted from his brother to the deputy procurator and up at Lenin, who did not look down from the picture behind the desk.

Felix did not smile. The terms had been made clear. Osip and Felix would continue to operate as long as it was safe for Khabolov. At the first sign of trouble, the deputy procurator would produce whatever doctored records he had prepared showing that he had conducted a patriotic investigation of their black market operation. He would turn in those whom it was safe to turn in and deny any allegations of payments in equipment or money from the lying black marketers, who would certainly be imprisoned, if they were lucky enough to make it to prison. Still, thought Felix, it was better than what they could be facing.

Being a Muscovite was dangerous at best. Better to be a wealthy Muscovite on the brink of disaster than a poor one.

"My son will be in touch soon," said Khabolov without rising, as he pulled the yellow pad back in front of him. "You are dismissed, Comrades, with the thanks of the state for your zeal in volunteering to serve."

"We are very honored..." Osip began as he rose, but Felix stopped him with a squeeze of the arm and led him out the door.

In the hall with the door closed behind them, Felix looked around to see if anyone could see them. When he was sure it was safe, he sagged against the wall and began shivering.

"We're safe," whispered Osip with a laugh. "Safe."

Felix looked at his brother, wanted to tell him how safe they really were, wanted to remind him that brother had denounced brother only moments ago, but he did not have the strength.

"Safe," he said, pushing himself away from the wall as two women in dark suits came around a corner talking and looking at them.

Felix moved on shaky legs to the elevator door with Osip at his side wanting to talk, celebrate. Felix didn't hear what Osip was saying. He looked back at the door to Khabolov's office, praying that it wouldn't open, that the deputy procurator would not come out, change his mind, ship them across Moscow to Lubyanka. When the elevator arrived, he hurried in past a uniformed officer and leaned against the rear wall. Osip had stopped talking but wore a relieved, happy smile that infuriated Felix, whose stomach tumbled as the elevator went down. He needed a toilet badly now, but knew he would not ask for one in Petrovka. Others got on the elevator and some got off. When they came to a sudden jerking stop at ground level, Felix felt like letting out a shriek of relief, but as the doors opened the thought of a shriek caught in his throat.

Standing ten feet away from the elevator, facing them, was a young man who seemed familiar. He wore a suit and carried a briefcase, and he looked directly at Felix and

Osip. And then Felix recognized him, the student who had bought the Beatles record the day before. What was he doing here? Was the world full of informants and policemen?

"We're free," Osip, hoarse, whispered as they strode toward the glass doors of the entrance past the armed guard.

"Yes," said Felix, looking back over his shoulder at the young man with the briefcase, who was watching the brothers move toward the door. "Free."

"Vadim Malkoliovich Dunin, you are relieved from duty," Rostnikov said to the young man who opened the apartment door.

Dunin was holding a teacup in one hand and the door handle in the other. Someone with a gun could have eliminated young Dunin and stained the floor of Katya Rashkovskaya's apartment with a single bullet.

"Yes, Inspector," Dunin said, stepping back to let Rostnikov in. "I have been unable to repair the toilet for Comrade Katya, but I did manage to turn off the water."

"Admirable," said Rostnikov, looking around for Katya. "Where is . . . ?"

"She went down the hall to a neighbor to use the toilet," Dunin explained, placing his teacup on the table and straightening his collar.

"You were supposed to remain with her." Rostnikov sighed.

"Even on the . . . ?"

"You could have waited in the hall. It doesn't matter. You are relieved. Now."

"My duty officer would like you to sign my report, Comrade Inspector," Dunin said, pulling out his notebook. "I've made my morning entry."

Rostnikov removed the books from under his arm, placed them on the table next to Dunin's cup, and reached for the report book.

"I didn't—" Dunin began.

Rostnikov held up a hand to stop him and signed his

name to the bottom of the report. He could have added a
slight reprimand, or a stiff one, for Dunin's lack of caution
in opening the door and his failure to stay with Katya. He
added nothing, but he looked at young Dunin's face when
he returned the notebook.

"Thank you, Comrade," Dunin said, aware that no written comments had been made by the inspector.

"You were lucky, Vadim Malkoliovich," said the inspector, with eyes fixed on the younger man's face.

"I know," agreed Dunin.

"You have an explanation?"

"None," said the young officer.

"Good," said Rostnikov, moving away to sit in a
straight-backed wooden chair. "There is hope for you."

Dunin smiled uncertainly and hurried out the front door.

For the first few minutes after Dunin's departure, Rostnikov sat looking around the room and waiting for Katya
Rashkovskaya to return. He knew from his previous visit
that it was a large apartment with two bedrooms. He knew
from previous experience that circus performers were
among the privileged, the lower privileged perhaps, but
privileged nonetheless. The furniture was comfortable,
rather modern, and, Rostnikov was sure, not cheap. He got
up and began to wander around, first looking at the
bathroom, where the toilet sat silent and wounded. Then he
moved to the small first bedroom, which held but a single
bed and was decorated with circus posters, colorful
posters, of clowns, bears, acrobats, dancers, elephants.
Each poster was covered by clear plastic, and if one were
to lie in the small bed one would be surrounded by a world
of color and movement. The single window in the room let
in a bright rectangle of sunlight that fell on the poster of a
man precariously balanced on five barrels. The man was
smiling, his arms outstretched. It was the room and poster
of the man who jumped from Gogol's head. No doubt. It
was not a woman's room, and there was something of the
energy of Valerian Duznetzov in the posters. Rostnikov
pulled open the top drawer of the dark dresser against the

wall and found his judgment confirmed by the clothes it contained and by an album of circus photographs, most of which included a smiling Duznetzov. The end of the book included many photographs of the beautiful Katya, whose smile, in contrast to Duznetzov's, was a mask. Rostnikov concluded that the third man in the photograph, the older bald man with the great chest, must be Pesknoko, the catcher.

"You find it interesting?" Katya Rashkovskaya said with irritation as he flipped to the final page of the album.

He had not heard her enter, a sign of her acrobatic lightness or his own age.

"Yes," said Rostnikov, without turning to look at the woman. "Interesting, sad."

He looked at the last page and slowly returned the album to the drawer.

"You frequently snoop in other people's drawers, the drawers of dead people," she said.

"Frequently," Rostnikov said, turning to face her. "It's my job."

"You enjoy it," she said.

"Usually," he agreed.

She stood in the doorway to the room, her arms folded in front of her once again, protecting herself. She wore a white dress and a light gray sweater, and her hair was loose and full around her face.

"It is an unpleasant job, a dirty job," she attacked.

"Sometimes unpleasant, sometimes dirty," he agreed, again moving toward her. She stepped out of the way as he approached and followed him as he moved to the other bedroom.

"What are you doing now?" she cried, as he opened the second door.

"My job," he said. "I'm trying to find out who killed Pesknoko and frightened Duznetzov to death."

The room he was in was larger than the other bedroom. No posters, but over the bed a large framed color photograph of Katya and Pesknoko in white tights. His arm was around her waist, and her smile, unlike that in the other photographs, was sincere. The blanket on the bed was a soft brown with a flower pattern and looked as if it might be silk.

"I don't want you looking in my drawers," she said.

"I won't."

Rostnikov glanced around the room and backed out into the living room, where he crossed to the small table.

"What do you want?" Katya demanded.

"I brought you the plumbing books," he said, handing her the books. "I also dismissed Dunin. The pistol I will have to keep."

She reached over to take the books from him, a quite puzzled look on her face. The man in front of her was an average-sized, dark crate of a man with a typical Moscow face: flat, dark-eyed, weathered. There seemed to be nothing unusual about him at first glance, but she could see a melancholy irony in his eyes as if he were about to tell a sad but poignant tale. And his words, his words were disarmingly honest. He was, she decided, a man to be wary of.

"Thank you," she said, taking the books and clutching them to her breasts as a schoolgirl would.

"I made a call before I came here," he said. "There is a small park on Leningrad Prospekt just past the airport."

"Near Alabyan Street?"

"Not that far, but you know the area. On the front page inside the book closest to your heart is the address and name of a woman who will get you a new toilet, will even have her sons deliver it if you can pay the price."

"I can pay the price," Katya said. "Thank you again. Do you want some tea, coffee?"

"No," Rostnikov said.

"Then?"

"I want," said Rostnikov, moving back to the wooden chair, "the name of the person you believe is responsible for the death of Oleg Pesknoko."

"Accidents," she said.

Rostnikov shook his head and looked at his short, knobby fingers laid flat on the table.

"I don't know," she said, angrily dropping the books on the table so that he had to pull his hands back quickly. "What do you want from me?"

"To save your life," he said, setting the books neatly and rising. "But I may not have the time. I am no longer investigating the accidents of yesterday morning. When I leave this apartment, the case will be closed, at least until whoever is responsible kills you."

His eyes met hers again, and she seemed on the verge of speaking but once again held back.

"Then there is nothing to be done," he said, moving to the door. "I'll return for the books in a week. I hope you are alive when I come for them."

"You are trying to frighten me," Katya said.

"Yes," Rostnikov agreed. "But I'm also telling the truth. I have a son in the army. He's just been sent to Afghanistan."

He had paused at the door to say this and turned for her reaction.

"I'm sorry, but . . . you are a confusing man. Why did you tell me about your son?"

Rostnikov shrugged.

"I don't know," he said. "I really don't. I thought it might somehow persuade you to let me help you. In my work there are far too many failures. Maybe it was as simple as thinking that my son would find you very pretty."

She smiled, showing even teeth.

"I like older gentlemen," she said teasingly.

"Pesknoko," he said.

The smile dropped from her face and she bit her lower lip.

"Yes," she said. "Why is this so important to you? Are you like this about all your investigations?"

"No," he said softly. "Perhaps it is the circus. Perhaps it is the memory of Duznetzov on Gogol's head, the rain splashing against his face. Perhaps it is simply you. I've never known anyone who has shot a toilet. It's an act of outrage I can understand."

Rostnikov left without another word. He had nothing

more to say. He walked slowly down the hall because his leg permitted him to walk no faster. He did not really expect that she would open the door and call him back, and she did not.

The morning was warm as Rostnikov crossed Lenin Prospekt and found a street bench from which he could see the entrance to Katya Rashkovskaya's apartment building. The bench was far enough away on the even-numbered side of the street so that she probably wouldn't notice him. Following her would not be easy. She was young, swift, an acrobat, but if she did not know she was being followed, he was confident that he could keep up with her.

Rostnikov looked up at the tall buildings and the sun, pulled a day-old copy of *Izvestia* from his coat pocket, and pretended to read as young mothers with baby carriages, old men heading for the park and each other, and *babushkas* with *avoskas* for shopping strolled past him. No one looked at him for more than a glance. It would be hours before anyone found it strange that this man had nothing to do for so long but read his paper. No one would bother him. They'd assume he was either a madman or a policeman and stay out of his way, but he preferred not to be noticed. As it was, he waited only seventeen minutes till Katya Rashkovskaya came through the entrance of her building. She did not look around to see if anyone were following her. She turned to her right and began to walk quickly away from Rostnikov's bench.

At this pace he was sure he would never keep up with her. There were no real crowds at this hour of the morning, so he would have trouble hiding, staying close. He stood up quickly, put his newspaper in his pocket, and turned to follow her at the same moment that a dark automobile pulled out of traffic, moved from the left lane into oncoming traffic on the right, shot across the street, and bumped over the curb toward the back of the unsuspecting Katya.

Rostnikov cupped his hands and bellowed above the sounds of traffic. His voice carried, heads turned to look at the madman, and one of the heads was that of Katya Rashkovskaya. An average person would have had no chance with the oncoming car, but Katya was an acrobat. She leaped backward instinctively, a graceful, high back flip that brought her down just beyond the fender of the dark car, which bumped over the curbing, missed an approaching bus, and joined the line of automobiles racing outward from the city.

Rostnikov lumbered forward, professionally stopping traffic with his outstretched hands as he had done as a young policeman. When he reached Katya's side, she was being comforted by an old woman who seemed to be no more than four feet tall and wore a black babushka over her head.

"Crazy mad," the woman said, holding Katya's hand. "A drunk. They tell us that all this drunkenness will stop, but does it stop?"

Katya was staring blankly at the building across the street.

"You poor . . . And the police. Where are the police? There used to be police everywhere," the old woman lamented.

"I'm the police," Rostnikov said.

The old woman looked at him as if he were drenched in acrid lemon juice.

"I'll take care of the young lady," he added.

Reluctantly, the old woman let go of Katya's hand, which, instead of falling to her side, remained extended as if still in the firm grip of the tiny woman.

"He could have killed her. You know that?" the old woman said, accusing Rostnikov.

"I know that," Rostnikov said, watching Katya's face. "I know that."

The old woman stood for a moment and then spotted someone not unlike herself across the street. She pulled herself away with a final shrug of disgust and hurried to tell the tale to her crony.

"I have nothing to say," Katya said through closed teeth, hyperventilating.

"This, too, was an accident?" he asked, ignoring the

pedestrians who slowed down to look at this frightened young woman and the barrel-shaped man.

"An accident," she said.

Summoning a hidden reserve, the young woman forced her eyes away from the building across the street, pushed away from the protection of the brick wall behind her, and looked at Rostnikov defiantly.

"An accident," she repeated.

"I cannot always be present to prevent accidents," he said.

"I know. *Spasee'ba*, thank you, but I'll do what I must do to see to it that there are no more accidents. You told me you were no longer investigating yesterday's... accidents."

"I'm not," Rostnikov said as she pulled herself together. "I'm now investigating a case of drunk driving and a near-fatal accident resulting from it. Premier Gorbachev wishes to eliminate drunkenness and I plan to help him. My first task will be to locate that drunk driver."

"You..." the young woman began and then changed her mind. She scanned the traffic coming and going, looked at the faces of people on the street, and hurried away much faster than Rostnikov could possibly follow.

Emil Karpo paused under the awning of a restaurant-bar off Kalinin Prospekt. The Belgorod was small and the service was poor even by Moscow's standards. The food was decent. The prices were not bad. There was no atmosphere to speak of, only a dozen tables in a dark main room and flimsy wooden tables with thick, brown, cotton cloths. The walls of the Belgorod matched the tablecloths, or came reasonably close, not by design but by chance. On the walls were indifferent paintings of imaginary landscapes. But most people did not come to the Belgorod for the food or the atmosphere. They came to discuss business, frequently illegal, or to meet one of the prostitutes who were known to check in with the bartenders and waiters.

The windows of the Belgorod were covered with lace curtains, making it impossible to see inside, though a bit of light managed to penetrate from the narrow street. It happened occasionally that a wandering tourist or a visitor from out of town might chance on the Belgorod and mistake it, because of the lace curtains, for a tearoom. Once he was inside, however, the smoke-filled room of suspicious-looking people would cause him to depart after fifteen or twenty minutes of nonservice.

Emil Karpo opened the door of the Belgorod and stepped into the near-darkness and the sound of voices. A man's deep, laughing voice turned into a cough. A woman giggled. It was still early, no later than noon, but every table was full, with couples and groups of men talking, drinking, leaning forward to conspire. A room of cheap suits and bright ties, made-up women. Several conversations stopped when Karpo entered, stopped because people looked up at the tall, pale figure whose head hardly moved but whose eyes looked them over and recorded them. The owner of the Belgorod was Serge Ivanov, who tended the bar. Normally Ivanov moved very slowly, as befitted an owner, but now he hurried toward his new customer and wiped his hands on his pants as he advanced with a little smile on his lips.

"Inspector," Ivanov whispered. He started to hold out a hand and then pulled it back. Ivanov was a thin man with a potbelly and a nervous twitch of the head that made it seem he was telling you to look to the right or that he was frequently saying no at the oddest of times.

Karpo said nothing.

"May I say," Ivanov began, the smile fixed, the head nodding, "I hope I can say, that I've known you long enough or at least been acquainted with you . . . The fact is that you are not . . . I mean, when you come in . . . How can I put this? My patrons, they feel, some of them feel a little uncomfort—. . . uneasy, when a policeman, you . . . You understand?"

"Mathilde," Karpo said, without looking at Ivanov. The policeman's eyes continued to scan the room. The noise level had dropped perceptibly since his entrance. A few men tried to engage him in a staring duel. Karpo paid no attention.

"Mathilde, as you can see," said Ivanov, looking around the room, "is not here today." He cleaned his palms once again against his trousers.

For the first time, Karpo looked into the eyes of the potbellied proprietor, and Ivanov wilted instantly.

"I'm just a small businessman," Ivanov bleated like a sheep. "I . . . in the back. A private party. What can I tell you? I forgot for a moment. It's been busy here like Bastille Day. Bastille Day is our busiest . . ."

Karpo moved past the tables of people who had been having a good time before his arrival and were now seriously thinking of all the work they had to do elsewhere. Ivanov followed him, smile fixed, head twitching.

"A small, private party," Ivanov said. "What's the harm?"

Karpo said nothing as he moved behind the bar and past a new waiter, who seemed about to step in front of the advancing ghost and then changed his mind.

"At least let's knock," said Ivanov, moving to Karpo's side. "It's only polite, reasonable, common courtesy to—"

Karpo reached down and opened the door with his left hand. The hand responded well, with little pain, and Emil Karpo was pleased.

The room he stepped into was remarkably large, almost as large as the outer room through which he had just come, but this inner room had only two tables and a dozen chairs. The tables were no more substantial than the ones in front, but they were larger. Two large blue sofas, badly contrasting with the brown walls, rested in the corner. The room reeked of tobacco and alcohol. There were only four people in the room when Ivanov and Karpo entered. They were seated at one end of the table farthest from the door. Two men and two women. The two men and one of the women looked up, surprised. The other woman glanced at Karpo and Ivanov and shook her head wearily.

"I tried," Ivanov said to the large man who stood up to face Karpo.

The big man had a pink face and a recent haircut. He was wearing an expensive jacket with medals. As he lumbered toward Karpo, the policeman could read the red enamel print on the largest medal: "Participant in the Achievements of the Economy of the Soviet Union."

"This is a private party," the big man said, clenching his fists. "I am drunk and this is a very private party."

"Inspector Karpo is a policeman, with the Procurator's Office," Ivanov said, his head twitching.

The big man did not seem impressed. His face was pink. He was drunk.

"I am an achiever," the big man with the pink face and fresh haircut said, thumping his chest with his already clenched fist. "My factory meets quotas and I'm on vacation."

Karpo ignored the man and took another step forward, which brought him almost face-to-face with the florid man, but the policeman was looking at one of the two seated women, a woman in her thirties, tall, with billowy brown hair, handsome, firm, but not quite pretty.

She shook her head, smiled without humor, and stood up.

"I'm talking to you," said the man with the pink face. "Policeman, I'm talking to you."

The woman grabbed her small bag and stepped around the table toward the policeman.

"There's no need—" Ivanov pleaded, grabbing the big man's arm.

The big man flung the owner away without looking at him. Ivanov stumbled to keep his balance and miss a nearby chair. He was either very graceful or very lucky, because he hit nothing and came to a stop not far from the wall, where he stood panting.

The woman walked past the two men to the door.

"I'm . . ." the big man said, grabbing Karpo's left arm.

"Boris!" cried the man who had not stood up, but Boris had gone too far to back down.

Pain ran through Karpo's arm and hand. The pain, like all pain, was good because it tested, confirmed, or denied.

By chance—luck, good or bad—the drunken man had grabbed Karpo at the most vulnerable point of his healing arm.

"...talking to you. Answer me, damn you. What are you doing here, breaking into a private—" The man stopped speaking when he realized that the gaunt, possibly insane, policeman had gripped his right arm just above the elbow. It was as if the policeman were about to embrace this man who was confronting him.

"There's no need..." Ivanov whimpered from the wall, afraid to step in again.

The other man at the table rose now. He was as clean-shaven as his friend, but was dark, not pink of face. He looked much more sober than did the man gripping Karpo's arm. The big man squeezed and Karpo tightened his own grip.

"Get out," said the big man to Emil Karpo.

Karpo said nothing.

The other man approached from the table and said, "Boris, this is ridiculous."

The woman who was still seated sat back to watch.

Karpo could see a half-finished bottle of Tvishi, a sulguni cheese that was definitely no longer hot, a bowl of red cabbage, and a large platter of what looked like chicken giblets on the table.

"Gentlemen!" cried Ivanov.

"Boris," whispered the other man.

The woman at the table reached over for a giblet, popped it into her mouth, and smiled at Karpo, who did not react. He felt nothing but the breath of the pink-faced man who panted like a hot terrier.

"Never," said Boris through clenched teeth. "Never."

Never came quickly. Boris suddenly let go of Karpo and backed away with a scream of pain that sounded something like "Ouosuch." He grabbed his arm where Karpo had squeezed it, grimaced, and stepped backward. The second man moved to help him. The seated woman continued to eat giblets, and Ivanov stayed out of the way. Karpo couldn't see Mathilde behind him at the door, but he was sure she had not left. He turned, ignoring the electric ache down the left side of his body and his left arm, and took a step toward her. Suddenly, behind him, he heard the pink-faced man plunging forward. Karpo turned to face him directly, to look into his eyes. What the charging man saw in Karpo's face was enough to put fear into him and send his alcohol-filled stomach tumbling. The big man stopped, stood panting, threw up his hands, which made him wince from pain, and turned back to his reduced party.

Mathilde led the way through the outer restaurant in which those patrons who had stayed after Karpo's entrance had been facing the private door and wondering. Mathilde and Karpo wound their way through the tables and out the door into the street.

"It's not Thursday," Mathilde said on the street, facing him.

"No," Karpo agreed.

For slightly over seven years, every other week on Thursday afternoon, Emil Karpo had come to Mathilde Verson, the prostitute. They seldom spoke. Even after all these years it was difficult for Emil Karpo to acknowledge what he did with her. It was not that the act of sex confirmed him as an animal, that much he knew and accepted. The animalism was a distraction, one his body would not let him deny. It got in the way of his duty, but it demanded that he respond, demanded that he acknowledge the un-asked-for ache, and threatened to keep him from his work. He acknowledged and controlled this need with Mathilde Verson. What bothered Emil Karpo was that his sexual encounters with Mathilde were illegal, counter to the needs of the state. The crime was not a particularly serious one, but the fact that it was a crime was a source of discomfort for Karpo. It also disturbed Karpo that he felt something beyond sexual need when he was with Mathilde.

Rostnikov, who knew about Mathilde, considered Karpo's reluctant acceptance of illegality one of the few antidotes for the hubris of the zealot.

"That was your bad arm he was playing with back

there," Mathilde said, walking by his side. "Are you all right?"

"Yes," he said.

"Yes," she repeated. "What else could I expect you to say?"

Two young women holding hands moved toward, around, and past the strange couple.

"I would like your help," Karpo said, looking ahead as they walked, feeling an electric sensation returning to his arm and side.

"I thought you only needed that once every other week," Mathilde said with a smile, looking at him.

Karpo did not smile back.

"You misunderstand," Karpo said.

"I was making a joke, Emil Karpo," she said, shaking her head.

"I see," said Karpo, flexing his fingers. He wondered, not for the first time, why people found it necessary to make jokes in his presence.

A man in a white shirt with an open collar glanced at the pale man flexing his fingers and then hurried past.

"What help do you want?"

"The prostitute killer," he said. "I may know who it is."

"Ah," she said as they walked.

"I know it is probably one of three people," he added as she paused to look into the window of a hat shop on Kalinin Prospekt.

"And how am I to help?" she asked.

"You want us to catch this killer," he said.

It was not a question, so she did not answer. She simply said, "I want you to catch the killer. I knew one of . . . I knew the second victim, Illyana Osnakovich."

"She was the third victim," Karpo corrected.

"An important revision," she said, still looking at the hats.

"It might be. Information must be kept in order or—"

"Do you like that hat?" she interrupted.

"That . . ." he said, looking at the red hat with the wide brim. "It does not look particularly functional."

"It is very functional," Mathilde said. "I would like that hat. You would like that hat on me."

"You are asking for a reward to do what you should do as a duty to the state," he said seriously.

"No," she said, squinting into the shop window and shielding her eyes with her hands to see if there were a salesperson inside. "I'll help, but I'd also like the hat."

"You'll have the hat," he said, wanting to massage his left arm with his right hand but resisting the urge.

"You plan to use me to lure this killer, to identify him when he tries to kill me."

"Yes," Karpo said.

A car skidded on the street somewhere behind them. They did not turn to look.

"It will be dangerous?" she asked.

"Perhaps," he answered.

"The red hat?"

"Yes," Karpo said, looking at her. "The red hat."

SIX

Maya held Pulcharia's cheek against her own as they stood in line in front of the shoe store on Gorky Street. She cooed something meaningless into the baby's ear and bounced her gently, almost backing into the couple behind her. The man was wearing denim pants, a checked shirt, and a white American cowboy hat. He had thick eyebrows and a thick beard. The woman was dark, thin, pretty, with long black hair. She carried a large colorful handbag that clashed with her blue-and-pink long skirt with a zigzag white pattern, which in turn clashed with the tight knit blouse with horizontal green stripes. The woman's shoulders were bare and brown.

"*Eezveenee't'e, pashah'lsta*," Maya said to the woman.

The woman smiled, brushed her arm where the baby might have touched her, and said, "It's nothing. The baby is very beautiful."

"Thank you," said Maya, looking at Pulcharia's sleeping face to reassure herself.

"I hear the shoes are Korean," the woman said.

"I heard Polish," said Maya.

"Polish," agreed the bearded cowboy.

The line moved forward, and Maya glanced across the street, where Sasha had been pacing as she waited in line. He should have been working. This was not a normal day off. He said that he had been assigned a new case, something to do with a gang of youths who were involved with some kind of extortion against shopkeepers beyond the Outer Ring Road. He shouldn't have come home to play with the baby. He shouldn't be pacing the sidewalk while she waited in line for a pair of Korean or Polish shoes. She wasn't sure they could afford shoes, but Sasha had absently told her to go ahead, get in line. They would manage.

Maya wanted to put the baby back in the buggy, but she was afraid Pulcharia would cry. The people in line would begin by being sympathetic and understanding and end by being irritable and giving her nasty looks. The morning was hot. The line was slow. The woman behind her was young and pretty, and Sasha was brooding. Maya reached back and pulled the buggy with one hand, holding the baby tightly with the other, as the line moved again.

Across the street, Sasha approached the cart of a white-clad ice-cream vendor, gave her some coins, and waited while she opened the metal door on her cart, reached in, and pulled out two ice-cream pops. Maya watched as he carefully crossed Gorky Street, dodging traffic. Maya watched him and was struck by the feeling that this moment had happened before. That she had stood here before now and that now the moment was happening again. Perhaps she had not stood here but had been a baby like her daughter and had seen her own father crossing the street with two ice creams. She knew the word for it, déjà vu, but this wasn't quite it.

"Ice cream," Sasha said, holding one out to her. "I read a report only weeks ago that said Muscovites eat a hundred and seventy tons of ice cream every day, summer and winter."

Maya took the ice cream and Sasha took the baby, who stirred drowsily. Sasha handed Maya his own ice cream and gently put the baby in the buggy. Pulcharia made an irritable sound, and Sasha began to rock the buggy with one hand as he took his ice cream back from Maya with the other. A *babushka* farther up the line turned around with a frown to see what was going on, saw the carriage, approved, and turned back to face the shoe store with her bag in her hand.

"I feel very old," said Maya after a small bite of the ice cream.

She looked back at the cowboy and the pretty girl in the clashing colors, who were engaged in a head-to-head whispered discussion.

"So do I," Sasha said. "The problem is that neither of us looks old or is old. It's a feeling that goes away."

"But it comes back," Maya said, taking another bite.

She had no trouble digging her teeth into ice cream, which sent a shiver down Sasha's back when she did it but also intrigued him, reminded him somehow of her independence, her strength. Maya's teeth were very good. His own were acceptable, except for the Romanian space between his top front teeth. His mother, Lydia, had the same space and she said that someone in each generation had it, that somewhere in antiquity there must have been a Romanian in her family. Sasha wondered if his daughter would have the space.

"You should be working," Maya said.

"I am working. That gang might be considering a move into the heart of the city, onto Gorky Street. I'm exploring that possibility," he said with a smile, trying to avoid being splattered by the ice cream, which had begun dripping in the late-morning heat.

Sasha looked at the pretty woman with the cowboy, and Maya saw him looking. Maya's and Sasha's eyes met and they both smiled. She handed him the stick from her ice cream. He took the last bite of his own, accepted her stick, and let her rock the buggy as he moved to deposit the sticks in the trash.

He wouldn't have the nerve to do what he was going to do without Rostnikov. Rostnikov seemed so confident, so quietly certain, not only that this was the proper course of action but also that it would work. Why Rostnikov should risk so much for him was something Sasha could not fully understand. Part of it, certainly, was Rostnikov's dislike for Deputy Procurator Khabolov, but something else was going on in the Washtub. Though he knew how to survive, there was a defiant, independent edge to the inspector that Tkach admired and feared.

"What?" Maya said as he returned to her in the line.

"What?" he repeated.

"What is wrong? Your eyes . . ."

"Work," he said. "The streets are full of criminals. If this line moves fast enough, you can put on your new shoes and we can walk to the park and lie in the grass. I don't have to be anywhere till noon."

"All right," she said. She felt better but not younger, for there was something in her husband's behavior that made her feel that this was a particularly important day and noon a particularly important time.

Dimitri Mazaraki parked his car and checked his watch. His schedule was off, and things were not going quite right. He had failed to hit Katya and he had seen in his rearview mirror the crippled policeman hurry across the street toward her. He got out, breathed deeply, touched his fine mustache, and grinned at nothing. He would survive, succeed. He had done so for this long. He would continue to do so. He was confident, sure of his cunning, his strength, his ruthlessness. He had no loyalty except to himself, and no dependencies. In Klaipeda, the coastal Lithuanian town on the Baltic Sea where he had been born and from which he had escaped through the *tsirk*, he had relatives—a sister, several cousins. He needed them and they needed him when he and the circus came to the area, but it was a need born of money and security, not of affection. As he had for years, Mazaraki had scheduled a circus tour to Lithuania and Latvia. The circus director had never questioned his scheduling, had even liked the idea, because he liked the Baltic beaches in the summer.

The tour would begin in a few weeks. Mazaraki was beginning to think that it would be his final tour to Lithuania. Killing Katya would, perhaps, give him time, enough time, but that policeman who loved the circus had unrelenting eyes. Mazaraki was sure about those eyes. He saw such eyes in his own mirror each morning when he admired his body and his fine mustache.

Mazaraki entered the New Circus building through the side door and moved toward his office. His footsteps echoed through the corridor that circled the building, and light streamed in from the tall, modern windows. Yes, he would get another chance at Katya, probably before the day was over, and if he did not he was fairly certain that she would say nothing, that she could say nothing. He had to, he would, protect himself.

- . And now he had work to do, a new act to schedule in, performers to talk to about extending their performances tonight to fill the show now that the Pesknoko act no longer existed. He would wear his red-and-black suit when he announced the acts. He would stand tall, meet the eyes of the crowd, introduce the performers as if he owned them, as if he were personally responsible for their very existences. It was a feeling he loved and would hate to lose. Perhaps, he thought, this will not be my last trip. It would be dangerous, but perhaps, just perhaps, he could keep it going for a while longer. In his office, Mazaraki checked his messages, found that the Circus School had called him about the act he wanted to recommend to the New Circus's director when he returned. Mazaraki sat behind his desk, surveyed his small office with satisfaction, and picked up the phone. Ten minutes later he had permission from the circus director, who was in Minsk, to bring in the new act at least on a temporary basis.

"Tragedy," said the director on the crackling phone line.

"Tragedy, indeed," echoed Mazaraki sympathetically.

"We'll have some kind of special dedication to Pesknoko and Duznetzov when I return," the director said. "What do you think?"

"An excellent idea, Comrade," said Mazaraki. "And I'll have the final tour plans ready."

"You are a zealous worker, Dimitri," the director said.

"I do my best," said Mazaraki, running his tongue over his white teeth as he examined his reflection in the window.

Five minutes later Mazaraki was in the locker/shower room in the rear wing of the building. He opened his locker, examined his black tights and short-sleeved black sweatshirt to be sure they were clean, and began to undress. Three men, the Stashov clowns, came in arguing. They were wearing loose-fitting work clothes and each was trying to outshout the other about some nuance of their act involving a pail of paint.

"Go back and see it again, and look carefully this time," said the oldest Stashov, the father. "Chaplin is handed the bucket. He doesn't bring it in."

"No, no, no. Never!" cried the middle Stashov, the one with red hair. "They do it to him. The old clown starts plastering him."

The middle Stashov was about to say something else but saw Mazaraki seated on the bench in the corner and shut his mouth. Mazaraki had that effect on the performers and was quite pleased with it.

"Comrade Mazaraki," said the Stashov father.

"Comrade Stashov," answered Mazaraki, putting on his American Puma shoes. "I have a videotape of *The Circus* if you want to see what Chaplin did. You can look at the scene in my office after I work out."

The Stashovs looked at each other furtively, surprised at this unexpected offer from the usually forbidding assistant director.

"We'd be very grateful, Comrade," said the older man.

"We are here to help each other," said Mazaraki, standing, a giant in black. "Like a big family."

"Yes," said the father with a nervous smile.

"Noon in my office," said Mazaraki, moving out of the locker room.

When he closed the door, the voices of the Stashovs resumed but they were quieter, wondering.

Mazaraki, back straight, walked across the hall to the rehearsal room where he had his weights. The sound of an accordion greeted him as he opened the door. The room was the size of a handball court, with echoes and cream walls. The carpet was green and thin. The accordionist was sitting on a pile of exercise mats in the corner. He wore street clothes and the red hat he used in his act. His partner, an incredibly beautiful thin young girl with long blond hair, sat beside him, her legs encased in tight jeans and pressed against the accordionist, who played and grinned at her. His teeth were too large. His face was also too large, but he had a way with bears and an act that always brought laughs. The girl was perfect for the act, a perfect contrast to both the bears and the homely accordionist. Mazaraki wondered what the girl thought when the accordionist made love to her. He wondered what it would be like to see the bear make love to her or to make love to her himself, balancing her on top of his flat, scarred belly.

The girl looked at Mazaraki and sensed something of his thoughts. She tugged at the sleeve of the accordionist, who had not looked up, and he pulled out of his reverie to smile at her and follow her gaze to Mazaraki. The music stopped.

"Go on playing," Mazaraki said, finding the chalk and powdering his palms.

"I was just . . . We were just finishing," the man said, his smile still fixed on his face but having lost its bemusement.

"Of course," said Mazaraki, looking at the girl, who pushed her long hair behind her back and avoided his eyes. The accordionist pretended not to notice the assistant director's look as he led the girl by the hand to the door.

"What was the song you were playing?" Mazaraki asked, reaching down for a pair of fifty-pound dumbbells.

"Just a . . . a French song," the accordionist said, opening the door.

"I like it," said Mazaraki, lifting a weight in each hand, feeling his biceps tighten. The girl tried not to look at him but turned and saw him grin under his huge mustache. She stared in fear and fascination for an instant before the accordionist led her out.

Alone, Mazaraki sighed deeply, straightened his back, and began to curl the dumbbells.

Ah, he thought, it feels good to be powerful.

The policeman had said something about lifting weights, Mazaraki remembered. The policeman, yes. Mazaraki was quite sure that he would be seeing that policeman again.

In less than a minute the sweat began to flow, and Dimitri Mazaraki sighed a sigh that echoed like the voice of a satisfied lover.

Rostnikov was looking at a book when Sasha Tkach arrived at the Gorgasali brothers' bookstall just off Lomonosov Prospekt. The crowd, mostly students carrying their own textbooks or purses, was large. Since it was noon, some of the people browsing chewed on sandwiches they carried or ate ice creams. The woman behind the flat table of books watched warily to protect her wares from theft and food stains. Sasha looked for the little girl who had been standing next to the trailer the day before, but she wasn't there.

"Sasha," said Rostnikov in greeting as he put down the book and limped away from the small crowd. The inspector hooked his arm around his young colleague and guided him to an open space where they could look across the university toward the Lenin Hills. On a clear day one could see the ancient and modern towers of Moscow across the hills and the Moscow River. This day was warm and clear.

"You know the history of the hills?" Rostnikov asked, looking toward the city.

"Somewhat, from school." Tkach pushed his hair back from his eyes. With Rostnikov he always felt as if he were a student about to learn some magical truth. He glanced through the crowd at the woman behind the tables to see if she recognized him, but she had no reaction.

"Look out there," Rostnikov said, biting his lower lip and shaking his head. "There's plenty of time. Some good will come of this day. I was following a young woman, thought I would not be able to join you, but she had no trouble eluding me. She was young like you, fast, a circus performer. You like the circus?"

Tkach looked at Rostnikov, whose eyes were fixed on the hills. If this conversation were going somewhere, its direction was a puzzle to Sasha, who wanted simply to turn and get their business over with. Rostnikov, however, appeared to be in no hurry and to have no interest in coherence.

"I haven't seen the circus since I was a boy," Sasha said.

"You'll want to take the baby there when she can understand, even before she can speak," Rostnikov said, sighing. "She may understand no more than the colors, the lights, the smells, but you will understand, will see the spectacle and see her wide eyes."

"I'd like that," said Tkach.

Rostnikov's eyes moved to the tall tower of the university.

"I would have liked Josef to go to the university," he said. "He would have liked it, too."

Sasha did not know what to say, so he said nothing as Rostnikov went on.

"The Lenin Hills used to be the Vorobyevy Hills, the Sparrow Hills, named for the village that used to be here. You knew that?"

"No, or if I did I didn't remember," said Sasha, looking back at the bookstall nervously.

"Patience, patience," said Rostnikov without looking at the nervous young man at his side. "A calm before we act. History has a calming effect. When I was a boy, I used to feel dwarfed by history, insignificant. I was nothing, a speck. That was what we were encouraged to believe and still are. I believed it. I still believe it. It frightened me as a boy, to be insignificant, one among millions and millions, lost in repeated history. And then one day, when I was almost killed by a drunk with a knife, I suddenly felt that the reason for my fear was the importance I attached to myself, my body, my thoughts. Are you following this?"

"I don't know," said Tkach.

Rostnikov patted him on the back.

"I've not gone mad. There's a point. Pay attention. I've not forgotten why we're here or why you think we're here. So, at the moment when I thought I was going to die I suddenly gave up any sense of the importance of my thoughts and body and I was set free. I was no longer bound by fear. Whatever I was, and I'm still not sure what that is, was, I knew, part of something far greater than I could understand. I was liberated by that moment, could smell, taste, feel, and not carry the burden of having to protect the fragile shell that, ultimately, I could not protect. And once I no longer protected, I could enjoy life. Food smelled better. My wife looked better. I loved my son without sadness. I could almost taste the iron when I lifted weights. Unfortunately, the understanding tends to fade a bit each day."

"I see," said Tkach with a nod.

"You mean you do not see." Rostnikov sighed. "All right. When I was sixteen a tank almost ended me and I had no revelation. Maybe it will come to you, maybe not. Let's go."

Tkach led the way around the book table to the rear of the trailer and knocked at the door.

"Who?" asked a quivering male voice.

"Police," said Rostnikov.

Another male voice inside the trailer muttered, "Oh, God. Oh, God," and the door opened. Rostnikov and Tkach climbed in and Tkach closed the door behind them.

The Gorgasali brothers were in approximately the same positions they had been in the last time Sasha had been in the trailer. The trailer seemed warmer this time, and Sasha was more aware of the smell of human sweat. He wondered if this warmth was harmful to the tapes in the cabinets.

The hairy younger brother was wearing a shirt and pants. The shirt was flapping out on the left side. His hair needed combing. The older brother sat behind the small table near the rear of the trailer, light coming through the heavily curtained window haloing his white mane. The older brother's face was pale with fear.

"You are a policeman," Osip said, looking at Tkach. "I saw you at Petrovka."

"We just said we were the police," Rostnikov reminded him. Then he turned to Sasha to add, "This is a man who would never understand the very hills on which he dangerously thrives."

"What? What did you say?" asked Felix, who was dressed as he had been at Petrovka: shirt, tie, jacket.

"We are here to save your lives," Rostnikov announced. "You would like your lives saved?"

Osip touched his stubbly cheeks with both hands, and his mouth opened to reveal teeth that should have been much better considering the money he and his brother apparently had made from their videotape operation.

"We are working for an important member of the Procurator's Office," Felix said, pale, veined, pulsing hands flat on the table. "We are patriots doing an important service for our—"

Rostnikov shook his head and Felix stopped.

"I have no time to play, no need to play with you," Rostnikov said, looking around the trailer. "Deputy Procurator Khabolov plans to become your partner, to share your profits, take home dirty American movies, and view them on the machines you will supply to him. When and if someone gets suspicious or he needs a success to save his job, he will turn the two of you in and you will be dropped into Lubyanka. No one will listen to your tale of betrayal. No one will believe it."

It was clear to Tkach from the faces of the Gorgasali brothers, particularly that of Felix, that this scenario was one that upset but did not surprise them.

Osip removed his hands from his face, hugged himself, and moaned as he looked at his older brother for help.

"I can't take any more," Osip groaned. "I'd rather be poor again."

"Why do you want to help us?" Felix asked, his voice thin and dry.

"Because if you go to Lubyanka," said Rostnikov, "my colleague here might go with you. Deputy Procurator Khabolov will need someone to blame for letting you operate after a report had been given. My colleague here would be the scapegoat, accused of being your partner."

"Now I understand," said Felix, blowing out a puff of air and reaching for a drawer. He opened the drawer and pulled out a half-full bottle of vodka. "Osip."

Osip nodded his head and for an instant didn't move. Then he roused himself and hurried to the front of the trailer, returning almost instantly with four glasses. He gave them to Felix, who began filling them.

"None for us," said Rostnikov.

Felix nodded and poured drinks for himself and his brother. Both brothers drank with trembling hands.

"What will we do?" asked Felix, pouring himself a second drink.

"You have equipment for videotaping?" asked Rostnikov, touching a metal cabinet nearby.

"Yes," said Osip, eagerly moving to a cabinet farther down, assuming the police would take the equipment as a bribe and go away.

"You know how to use it?"

"Yes," said Felix, perhaps beginning to understand.

"Good," said Rostnikov. "Good. Show us."

For the next half hour Osip demonstrated how to use the Japanese equipment. Rostnikov paid little attention but knew that Tkach was absorbing everything. The inspector was deciding how to set the scene, where to put the blankets. Felix watched him while Osip spoke, partially losing his fear in his absorption with the machines.

"I know what you plan to do," said Felix as he downed his fourth glass of vodka. His gray face was perspiring, his mane of hair limp. "It could fail, get us all killed very quickly."

"Or it might succeed," said Rostnikov. "Success, failure, quickly, or a slow wait till the inevitable moment when the knock on the door will not be from two policemen who have an interest in saving you."

". . . the tape for longer periods," Osip was saying as Rostnikov turned.

"Sasha," Rostnikov interrupted, "I've got to go find the circus woman. You finish here and tell these gentlemen what they must do next."

Tkach looked at him steadily and nodded. Rostnikov patted his friend's shoulder and went through the side door of the trailer and into the sun.

Yuri Pon was not having a good morning. First, his head hurt, a pulsing pain the source of which was surely the vodka he and Nikolai had drunk the night before. There had been too many nights like this recently. At first the idea had been to dull Yuri's nights, get him through without the dreams, the images, the longings. But last night he had simply drunk to blot out Nikolai's snoring. Yuri had already decided that he had to find another prostitute, had already met with enough failure. He needed a clear head tonight if he were to find one, to get some relief.

Second, while he had concluded that whoever had looked at the file on the eight killings the day before had probably only been involved in a routine check on something else, he could not really be sure. Inspector Karpo had made no appearance, had given no further evidence of his interest in the file.

Third, the small screw on the right side of his glasses was loose, very loose. He had tried to tighten it with a tiny screwdriver but it barely held, and every hour or so it needed tightening again. Getting his glasses repaired or replaced would be hell, take days. He took them off for the fifth time that morning and tried to tighten the small screw with his thumbnail. It moved a bit.

Fourth, Ludmilla Kropetskanoya, that dark pole of a creature, had dumped extra work on him, had told him to begin the end-of-the-year inventory and cost projections for paper, folders, and nonhardware items. That should be her job, not his. Couldn't she see, didn't she know after all these years, that the efficiency of the files was his doing? Wasn't it evident to her that all the computerizing of files was on schedule because of Yuri Pon? By the end of the current year, if he were not bothered with tasks that could be done by a bookkeeper, and if he were allowed to keep the three clerks who were assigned to the task, he would have all files transferred to the computers.

"... if we keep down the order for manila twos because we won't need them when we turn to the computers," she said, leaning over Yuri, her foul breath in his ear. What did she eat each morning? What rotting fish clung to her yellow teeth?

"I thought we were going to maintain the paper file system as a backup," he said, twitching his nose to push his glasses back. He wanted to push her back, away. God, how his head screamed.

"The latest thinking is that there will be no need for written files at all," she said. "Backup tapes will be kept. Our primary job will be to copy the written reports into the computers, file them properly, and destroy the paper."

"I see," said Yuri, but he didn't see. He didn't see why he had to be told this way, told so casually, that his records, the records he had worked on for more than half his life, were to be destroyed and that he was going to be turned into a way station between policemen and a computer. There was no art to that, no skill. He could see that the computers were more efficient, but there were nuances one couldn't program. He had seen them, the way an officer wrote something, emphasized it by bearing down, or the space that was taken, the size of the letters. One could tell something by the writing, the individuality. Each report was different, but they would all seem the same on the computer: each letter the same size, each line the same length, only material programmed that could be retrieved.

"I see," he repeated, but if his glasses fell off, if his head began to hurt any more, if this feeling of rage and the need for relief were not controlled, he would be able to see nothing.

"Good," she said with no further explanation as she left for her office.

Yuri was sweating, his hands folded in his lap, as he

looked at the long inventory sheet Ludmilla had placed on
the desk in front of him. He got up and walked around the
row of file cabinets that stretched for fifteen rows. In the
corner, where he couldn't be seen, Yuri sat at the computer
terminal, closed his eyes, and clenched his teeth. The
clenching brought more pain to his head. He opened his
eyes, turned on the machine, listened to it hum to life, and
punched in the file number he wanted, the one for the serial prostitute killings. Then he called up the file itself and
watched the names and reports go by, letting each name,
each situation, recall the feeling.

Ludmilla, Nikolai, his own mother, thought of Yuri as
an almost fat, dull minor bureaucrat. He was that. He knew
he was that and he didn't mind, but he was more. He had
watched for years as the state did nothing about these
women, these women he saw everywhere. He, Yuri Pon,
whom no one thought of. Ha, he didn't even think of himself. He, Yuri Pon, was slowly, systematically, ridding
Moscow of a class of criminals. Jack the Ripper, the En-
glishman, seemed to have had something of the same idea.
Jack had succeeded in changing some things, bringing
down a corrupt police system. Yuri had read about him.
The same thing would happen for him. The city would
have to recognize the existence of prostitution, do something about it as he was doing.

The feeling he had when he did it, stalked, found, was a
patriotic frenzy. He couldn't deny its sexuality but he
didn't have to admit it, either. Oh, God, tonight. It would
have to be tonight. He couldn't wait. And then he stopped,
his eyes fixed on the screen, the words before him. Someone had recently called up this file. That was normal, but
the system showed a cross-check file still in the computer.
Someone had coordinated data from other files with this
one. Yuri pressed the indicated code and the letters on the
screen began to roll down. It was a series of names, five
names, and the personnel coordinates on each, including
days off for illness, nonworking days, hours worked each
day. One of the names was his.

Someone had linked Yuri's name to the file, to the killings, but who and why? It was the same person who had pulled the paper file on the case, his file. It must be Karpo. It was not a routine check. There was no initial on the access code, though there was supposed to be. Everyone, including filing personnel, was supposed to initial any program or any use of a program. He sat looking at his name on the gray screen, and then methodically, letter by letter, the file began to disappear. Yuri looked back over his shoulder. There was no one there. He looked at the screen, panting. Someone, somewhere, was erasing the file that included his name on a list. Someone had seen what he wanted to see and now was eliminating the information. Yuri wanted to climb into the screen, follow the wiring, be led by electricity, until his own face appeared on the screen in front of whoever was doing this. He wanted to look at that face, frighten it with a grin. He put his hand on the screen to slow down the *ping-ping-ping* removal of each letter. Then his name started to disappear, N-O-P-I-R-U-Y. It was followed by the others, and then the screen was blank, the computer humming.

Yuri looked at his watch to see how many more hours he had to work. Seven. His glasses fell from his nose and clattered to the floor.

From beyond the files, somewhere near his desk, the voice of Ludmilla Kropetskanoya called irritably, "Comrade Pon, where are you?"

The walk from the Gorgasalis' trailer to the New Circus was a short one, but Rostnikov had taken it slowly, pausing frequently to rest his aching leg. He arrived just before noon and was let in by the same old man who had let him in before.

"You're the policeman," said the old man, who clutched a mop in his left hand.

"I'm the policeman," Rostnikov confirmed. "I'm looking for Katya Rashkovskaya. Have you seen her?"

"The flyer?"

"The flyer," Rostnikov confirmed.

"I'm not sure," said the old man. "Might have been this

morning. Might have been yesterday. I think it was today. I think it was just a little while ago. When you do the same thing every day, it's sometimes difficult to tell one day from the other."

"Yes," agreed Rostnikov as he watched the old man dressed in gray work clothes try to remember on which day he had seen the woman. "Assuming it was today, where did you see her?"

The man smiled and pointed upward with his free hand.

"Going to the offices, not rehearsal rooms, not the ring," he said. "Performers don't practice as much today as they did when I was a performer."

Rostnikov waited for the man to tell him more, but the old man was leaning on his mop, his eyes far away, remembering some old day, some old act. Rostnikov walked in the direction of the nearest stairway and started up slowly. A chattering family—mother, father, young girl, and boy—all dressed in blue suits, came hurrying down the stairs. Rostnikov moved to the side to let them pass.

On the second floor above the lower corridor Rostnikov found a series of offices. There was the distant echo of music deep inside the building and the sound of a woman's voice. Rostnikov followed the voice and not the music and found himself in front of a solid wooden door marked in black letters: ASSISTANT TO THE DIRECTOR.

He paused, tried to listen, but could make out only the voice and not the words. There seemed to be an edge of hysteria to the voice. Rostnikov knocked and the voice stopped. He knocked again and the door opened.

Facing him was Mazaraki, who grinned broadly and stepped back to let him enter. In a corner stood Katya Rashkovskaya. She was not grinning broadly. She was not grinning at all.

"*Tavah/reeshch*, Inspector," Mazaraki said a bit too loudly. "It is good of you to visit us again. To what do I owe the pleasure of your return?"

Rostnikov looked at Katya, whose knuckles were white against her oversize purse. Her eyes met his but showed less than her pink cheeks. Porfiry Petrovich turned to Mazaraki with new interest. Mazaraki looked just as big as the detective had remembered him, but was there not a dancing in his eyes as if the moment were of great consequence?

"I was looking for Comrade Rashkovskaya," Rostnikov said, watching the smiling mask of a face of the assistant director.

"Fortuitous," Mazaraki said, leaning back against his desk and folding his hands across his chest.

"Perhaps," agreed Rostnikov. "I would have been here earlier but I no longer have access to an official automobile. I have to take a bus or the metro or, in an emergency, a taxi. Do you have an automobile, Comrade Mazaraki?"

"Yes, a little Moskvich," answered Mazaraki, his head tilted slightly to the right like a curious bird. "Very economical."

"It's important to drive carefully," Rostnikov said, looking around at the office. "May I sit?"

"Please," said Mazaraki, unfolding his arms and waving an open hand at a dark wood-and-leather chair.

Rostnikov moved the chair slightly, just enough to be able to see both Katya and Mazaraki at the same time. And enough to survey the room, which was furnished in dark wood and leather, like something out of a magazine. The desk was large and a television sat on the wide lower level of the bookcase along with a machine that was attached to it and that Rostnikov assumed was a videotape player.

"I have a modest collection of films, Inspector," said Mazaraki, moving to the bookcase cabinets and opening one. "Even some American films, which I trust are not illegal to own."

"I'm not interested in legal or illegal movies," Rostnikov said, looking at the neat row of tapes. He wondered if Mazaraki were a client of the Gorgasali brothers, whose trailer was less than a mile away. Perhaps he would find out.

"I've got Keaton, Chaplin, *Grease, Gone With the Wind, Blue Thunder,* even *Raiders of the Lost Ark,*" said Mazaraki.

Mazaraki was running his large right hand over the

tapes and looking over the policeman's head at the silent woman, who remained motionless in the corner.

"Someone in the MVD has the idea that Pesknoko was murdered," Rostnikov said, watching Mazaraki's eyes, which remained on Katya, revealing nothing. His lips, however, tightened.

"Someone?" said Mazaraki, closing the cabinet and moving his right hand up to play with his mustache. He pulled a longish patch above his lip downward and bit at it with his teeth.

"Someone," Rostnikov said, examining his lap.

"You?"

Rostnikov shrugged. It was a possibility.

"And you are investigating?"

"No," sighed Rostnikov. "The case is closed. I am investigating a hit-and-run this morning. It seems Katya Rashkovskaya was almost killed by a motorist outside her apartment building."

"No," said Mazaraki, moving behind his desk and looking up at Katya. "Katerina, you said nothing. After all that has happened, this is quite terrible."

Rostnikov turned awkwardly, deliberately, to face the young woman, who still had not spoken.

"You had other things to discuss," said Rostnikov. "Business, Katya's future."

"Yes," said Mazaraki behind him.

The young woman nodded yes.

"Is it not a bit unusual," continued Mazaraki, "that a full chief inspector is investigating a drunken driver who accidentally—"

"Your car is parked outside?" Rostnikov cut in.

Mazaraki's smile disappeared for an instant and then returned, more fixed, more artificial, than before, the broad smile of a performer who wanted the smile to be seen forty rows back in dim light.

"My car is parked outside," Mazaraki said, playing with his mustache.

"Well, this has been an interesting, though brief, visit," Rostnikov said, using both arms of the chair to raise himself. "Comrade Rashkovskaya, if you are finished here, perhaps I could have a few words as you walk wherever you—"

"I'm going home," she said softly, her eyes turning away from both men.

"Good," said Rostnikov. "We can talk on the way."

Mazaraki rose quickly and hurried around the desk and to the door to open it.

Rostnikov looked up at the bigger man as Katya stepped into the hall.

"Would you like to see the circus tonight, Comrade Inspector? As my personal guest?"

"I like the circus," said Rostnikov, looking into the hall at the woman, whose eyes were fixed on the big man.

"I'll leave your name at the box office. Would you like to bring—?"

"My wife and I would very much like to see the circus," Rostnikov cut in.

Mazaraki bowed his head slightly, perhaps mockingly.

"I would like to see you working," said Rostnikov. "I have the impression that you are an outstanding performer."

"Thank you, Inspector," Mazaraki said, and Rostnikov stepped into the hall. The door closed slowly behind him.

In the hall, he caught up with Katya.

"You'll have to walk more slowly if I'm to keep up with you."

"I'm sorry. I really don't want company."

"You might find it comforting, protective."

"I need no comforting or protection," she said, increasing her pace.

At the bottom of the steps, about ten feet below him, she stopped and turned.

"I will take care of my business," she said.

"I am a patient policeman," Rostnikov said softly so she would have to strain to hear him. "At some point I will hear this story. I prefer to hear it from you, but if you are not around to tell it, I will hear it nonetheless."

"Thank you for the plumbing books," she replied and

hurried to the front door past the old man with the mop. Her hard heels clacked and reminded Rostnikov of some piece of music, the memory of which passed almost as quickly as it had come. He watched her go out the door into the sunlight and turn to her right.

"She's good," said the old man as Rostnikov limped forward.

"I know," said Rostnikov.

"You've seen her?" asked the old man.

"No."

"Then, how . . . ?"

"Where does the assistant director park his car?"

The old man looked at Rostnikov with uncertainty, but answered. "Back behind the building. There's a small lot. His space is right near the door."

"Thank you," said Rostnikov, turning toward the rear of the building.

He found the rear door with no trouble. And the car. It was black. As he stepped into the lot, he looked up at the side of the building and found the window of Mazaraki's office. He had thought for a moment that Mazaraki's office was farther down a bit, but the angry, smiling face of Dimitri Mazaraki, his arms folded, framed in the window, made it evident that Valerian Duznetzov had made a slight drunken mistake before he leaped from Gogol's head. It was not a man who saw thunder whom he feared but a man who saw *Blue Thunder*.

SEVEN

WHEN ROSTNIKOV STEPPED AROUND THE BUILDING onto the sidewalk of Vernadksogo Prospekt, he knew he would not have to walk to the metro station. The black Volga with the darkened windows was a symbol. The heavyset man in the blue suit leaning against it was a sign, a sign he recognized. The man was smoking a cigarette. He looked at Rostnikov without emotion or a nod, and Rostnikov walked slowly toward the man and the car.

No one spoke as the man opened the car door and Porfiry Petrovich got into the back seat. A trio of young women tried not to glance at the KGB vehicle, laughed a bit too heartily at nothing, and moved quickly on. The seat was clean and soft and the car smelled of tobacco. Rostnikov did not recognize the driver. However, the man who had been leaning against the car was one of the two he had encountered yesterday in the lobby of the hospital where he had met with Drozhkin.

Rostnikov did not enjoy the ride. He did not dread it, but he did not enjoy it. He looked out the window, wondered if it would rain, wondered if he would be finished with whatever they were going to do with him in time for him to get Sarah and go to the circus. For a flash of time too thin to grasp, he even wondered if they were going to take him to a place where he would never see his wife, his son, or the light of day again. The thought, or fragment of thought, did not frighten him as much as it scratched him with a shudder of curiosity.

The ride took less than twenty minutes. They rode on large boulevards in the center lane—reserved for party members, the KGB, and dignitaries with special connections. The car pulled up to the door of the small hospital and Rostnikov was escorted inside by the burly KGB man. They were met by the second big man, in an identical blue suit, and once again they moved past the desk, to the elevator, and up to the patio, where his escorts remained in the hall as he stepped outside.

A slight wind was blowing as late afternoon approached. Drozhkin was seated in the same chair, almost in the same position, under the fifth canopy. His eyes were open and watching as Rostnikov limped forward.

"You are looking better, Colonel," Rostnikov ventured.

"It is an illusion," said Drozhkin, his gray hand reaching for a drink of what looked like lemonade. "I am much worse, worse by the day. Would you like to sit?"

"Yes," said Rostnikov.

"Well, you may not do so," said Drozhkin. He sucked at a glass straw in the drink, his cheeks drawing in, his face showing what his skull would soon look like. "Do you know why?"

"You wish me to be uncomfortable, Comrade," answered Rostnikov.

"Yes, I wish you to be uncomfortable." Drozhkin looked at the drink with distaste and put it down. "You have made the last several years, the last years of my life, uncomfortable. You do not listen to what you are told. You don't seem to understand the consequences of your rebelliousness. You have stepped into at least five situations in which you interfered with our work. You know that?"

Rostnikov shifted his weight, trying to ignore the discomfort that would soon become pain.

"It is difficult always to avoid the jurisdiction of the KGB, Comrade," he said. "The lines are not always clear and . . ."

Drozhkin started to reach for the lemonade again and changed his mind. The effort was too great. A sudden breeze whipped his gray hair into a frenzy and settled again.

"This had nothing to do with lines," the old man said. "I told you to stay away from the circus investigation. You remember I told you that?"

"I remember, Comrade," said Rostnikov. "I have given up that investigation."

"Then why did you follow the woman? Why did you go to the circus? I don't expect the truth, but I do expect a story that will not make me think you a fool or, worse, make me think you take me for a fool."

"I was investigating a hit-and-run case, or almost a hit and run. The victim was—"

"The Rashkovskaya woman," Drozhkin said, sighing.

"Colonel Snitkonoy is aware of my—" Rostnikov began again, only to be cut off by Drozhkin.

"The Gray Wolfhound is a fool. I'm a dying man. I need no longer be politic. He is a fool. You know it. I know it. What is this suicide urge you possess, Porfiry Petrovich?"

The familiarity startled Rostnikov, who feared that his leg was about to give way. He examined the old man, who was shaking his head and looking at him. Drozhkin smiled, the smile of a ghost, but a smile. Rostnikov smiled back tentatively.

"It's a good thing I'm dying, a good thing for both of us," said the old man. "I'm afraid I'm beginning to understand you, and that might lead to liking you, and that would not be a good thing. But if you keep up behavior like this, I may yet outlive you."

Rostnikov said nothing. He knew that in a few minutes he would begin to sway and that if he did not sit down or at least lean against something he would run the risk of collapsing.

Drozhkin reached for the half-filled glass of lemonade

again, picked it up, looked at it with disgust, and threw it to the wooden floor. Shards rained on Rostnikov's trousers, and the two burly KGB men burst through the door with pistols leveled at Porfiry Petrovich.

"I dropped a glass," Drozhkin said, without looking at the two men, his watery eyes on Rostnikov. "Tell the nurse to come out here and clean it up when the inspector and I are finished."

The two men departed, closing the patio door behind them.

"You look uncomfortable," said Drozhkin, pulling a knit blanket over his knees. "Imagine what it is like to have this thing eating inside me. That is uncomfortable. You think I'm complaining?"

"No," said Rostnikov.

"Sit down, damn you. Sit down."

Rostnikov moved forward slowly to the wooden chair and sat. His leg was stiff and straight, and he knew better from thirty-five years of experience than to try to bend it.

"You are supposed to thank me," said Drozhkin. He threw his hands up and shook his head. "What's the use? You must stay away from the circus, from Mazaraki, because we are watching him. We know he killed Pesknoko. We know he drove that drunken fool to jump off the Pushkin statue."

"It was the Gogol he jumped off," Rostnikov said.

"The Gogol, then. All right. What's the difference?"

A great deal, thought Rostnikov. But he said nothing.

"Mazaraki has been using his tours of the socialist states to smuggle people over the borders to the West," said Drozhkin. "They pay massive amounts, these storekeepers, black marketers, Jews, and he gets them to the borders and often beyond as troupe members, one at a time, sometimes two. He has relatives in Latvia or Lithuania who help him. I can't remember which. Just four or five a year smuggled out for the past six years has made him wealthy."

"I've seen his office," Rostnikov said.

"Duznetzov, Pesknoko, and the woman were part of his scheme," explained Drozhkin. "He needed them to help him cover. At one level a brilliant idea. Circus performers don't defect. Their lives here are good, secure. They travel, live well, get lifetime pensions when they retire. But once in a while a Mazaraki comes along, a Lithuanian or Latvian with desires for more. I'm getting tired."

"I'm sorry," said Rostnikov.

Drozhkin looked at his guest, his thin, cracked lips tight.

"You say that with insufficient conviction."

"I'm sorry. I was distracted for a moment thinking about my son."

"Ah, the son," Drozhkin said with understanding. "You raised the stakes, Porfiry Petrovich. You tried to play in blackmail against me. It was a game of cards and I called your bluff."

Rostnikov said nothing and then, "So you want me to stay away from Mazaraki so you can trap him when he goes on his next tour?"

"That broken glass there is dangerous," Drozhkin said, his voice cracking. "All I need besides what I have is a foot full of glass." Then he looked up at Rostnikov. "No, you do not understand. We want Mazaraki to continue to smuggle people out of the Soviet Union. If you must know, we have even subsidized him without his knowledge. Are you beginning to understand?"

"He is smuggling some of your people out, undercover defectors," said Rostnikov, making the first attempt to move his locked leg and finding it most difficult.

"Something like that," agreed Drozhkin. "The price we pay in letting a few *nakhlebniki*, parasites, intellectuals, run away is worth what we gain in the long run but . . ."

"Mazaraki is becoming a bit unstable," said Rostnikov.

"He seems to be going mad," agreed Drozhkin. "It's not surprising. Six years of what he has done. Duznetzov cracked under the pressure. I don't know about Pesknoko. My guess is that Mazaraki got rid of him because he feared he would not make it."

"The woman," said Rostnikov.

"The woman, yes," said Drozhkin, pulling the blanket up to his waist. "It's getting cold here."

"Yes, it's getting cold," Rostnikov agreed, feeling quite warm.

"The woman is the least likely to crumble, but Mazaraki does not understand that and so he feels he must get rid of her."

"And we," said Rostnikov, finally bending his knee, "must not stop him."

"He must make the next tour, at least the next tour," whispered Drozhkin with a shiver. "His cargo is especially valuable to us. I'm tired now. I must sleep. You must stay away."

"You work to the end," Rostnikov said, rising.

Drozhkin's eyes were closed, and Rostnikov could not hear what the old man mumbled.

"I'm sorry. . ." Rostnikov said.

"I said," Drozhkin groaned dryly, "you would do the same. I will die loyal to the revolution. I don't know what your motives would be. Tell them to send in the nurse when you leave."

"I will, Comrade," Rostnikov said, moving toward the door.

Colonel Drozhkin said nothing. His eyes remained closed. His thin right hand rose slightly from the blanket in what might have been a wave of good-bye or a sign of dismissal.

Rostnikov moved slowly past the two KGB men after telling them the colonel wanted a nurse. One of the men, the one who had come with him in the car, escorted Rostnikov to the lobby and out of the hospital. The other man hurried for the nurse.

In the street, Rostnikov moved for a waiting taxi nearby. He could not make it to the metro or the bus. He would file for reimbursement. Perhaps the Wolfhound would grant it, perhaps not.

He should have gone back to Petrovka. He went over what he had been told by the dying colonel. It was simple. He was to stay away and let Mazaraki kill Katya Rashkovskaya. He was to stay away or else. Rostnikov suddenly felt hungry, very hungry, hungry as a snarling bear. He gave the driver his address on Krasikov Street and closed his eyes.

Deputy Procurator Khabolov smoothed back his hair with both hands and examined his teeth in the mirror of his beloved white Chaika. The car was almost like new in spite of the recent damage that was done when the vehicle had been stolen. The damage had been repaired by a disreputable mechanic known as Nosh, the Knife, who owed much, including his freedom, to the deputy procurator.

It was early in the afternoon, a sunny afternoon, and Khabolov felt confident as he stepped out of the car, locked it carefully, pulled the chain around the door handles and inserted the padlock. He snapped the padlock after checking his pocket for the key and moved to the trailer of the Gorgasali brothers. It looked a bit smaller than he had expected, but he had hopes, hopes for the best. It had been a good year for Khabolov, a good year indeed. First, Anna Timofeyeva had been stricken with a series of heart attacks to open the deputy procurator's position for him at the very moment when Odessa had grown too small for him. And then Rostnikov, who always looked as if he had some secret joke and seemed to be saying more than his words, was transferred to the MVD. It had something to do with some trouble with the KGB. Khabolov didn't care. Rostnikov, with his knowing eyes, was gone. And then this, this had fallen onto his desk.

In thanks to the God his father back in Odessa still believed in, Khabolov would give the old man a videotape machine and a supply of movies for his forthcoming eighty-first birthday. Yes, it would be a token of Khabolov's humility, his gesture to show that he still revered and respected his father. It would also give his father, whose respect for his son was too often minimal, further evidence of how wealthy and powerful his son had become.

Khabolov adjusted his glasses, tightened his tie, and knocked once, hard, at the door to the trailer. The door opened almost immediately. He was sure they had been waiting for him, watching him arrive in his Chaika.

"Comrade Procurator," Felix Gorgasali said, ushering him in. "We are honored."

Gorgasali backed away as Khabolov entered with a wave of the hand, indicating that he accepted the thanks.

The trailer was a bit bigger inside than the deputy procurator had expected, but the line of metal cabinets was promising. Since he had never been in the trailer before, he thought nothing of the curtained area in the front of the vehicle. He was also unaware that the interior of the trailer was normally much darker than it was now, with powerful 300-watt bulbs in each outlet.

"Comrade Procurator," said Osip Gorgasali, rubbing his hands and stepping forward. It looked as if he were about to extend his hand to shake and then thought better of it.

"I have very little time," Khabolov said, looking around the trailer, adjusting his glasses, and taking a notebook out of his inner jacket pocket. "Give me a quick inventory, in general terms, with the names of clients to whom you have sold equipment and tapes."

The brothers looked at each other. The dark younger one with the balding head looked toward the front of the trailer and then at his brother, who said, "Most of our customers don't give names, and we don't ask them, do we, Osip?"

"No," said Osip. "We don't ask them. We should, but we don't. We'll start asking them right away. Today."

"Good," said Khabolov. "The names are especially important."

"There will be names," promised Felix.

The two brothers seemed nervous, but nervous was the only way Khabolov had ever seen them, nervous and frightened, which was just the way he wanted them.

"A rough inventory now," Khabolov said, moving behind the table and sitting with his pad and pen. A rough inventory is what he got. Ten minutes later the deputy procurator said "Good" and stood up.

"Thank you, Comrade," Osip said. "If there is anything, anything . . ."

"Yes. I will have to take two video players and a television set, plus twenty, no, twenty-five, tapes. I've written the titles on this sheet."

He tore off a sheet from his notebook and handed it to Osip, who handed it to Felix. Khabolov closed the notebook and returned it to his pocket.

"May we ask? I mean you are going to do . . . something with these tapes and the machines," said Felix through a close-toothed smile.

Khabolov adjusted his glasses and gave the man a withering glare, a glare over his nose that he had spent nearly twenty years developing, a glare that said, "How dare an insignificant bit of cheese like you ask a question like that of someone as important as I?"

"I just . . ." Felix whispered, backing away.

Khabolov took a step toward him, his eyes meeting the frightened, watery eyes of the elder Gorgasali brother.

"The white Chaika outside is mine. The trunk is open. Put it all in the trunk," he said.

Felix gulped and nodded to his brother. Khabolov did not remove his eyes from Felix's, but he heard Osip clumsily open cabinets, move, find.

"What I do with this," Khabolov said, patting the notebook in his pocket, "and with you, is entirely up to me. I can use you, your equipment, your tapes, in any way I choose. To catch economic traitors to the revolution"—with this he paused to make it clear who two such economic traitors might be—"to give to my friends, or to use myself. Each day of freedom for the two of you is one more day than you should have."

Felix closed his eyes, opened his mouth, opened his eyes, and in a voice filled with fear croaked, "But you would be in trouble if you used any of this for your own profit and Osip and I told about it during an inquiry."

Khabolov smiled, a small rodent smile that he thought made him look like the villain in a decadent French play he had once seen. He enjoyed a small display of rebellion, one that could easily be crushed.

"I would call you a liar," Khabolov said, grabbing Felix's tie. "I would call you a liar and accuse you of the most obscene of crimes, crimes for which I would produce great mounds of evidence, sacks and boxes of evidence. You would both choke on the evidence. Do you understand? Do I make myself clear?"

"Yes, yes, yes," croaked Felix, his white hair falling over his eyes.

Khabolov let go of Felix's tie, removed a handkerchief from his pocket, wiped his palms to cleanse them from the contact, and replaced the handkerchief without removing his eyes from the cowering peddler. Khabolov was proud of his performance and thought of how nice it would be to have someone witness it who would really appreciate his artistry.

"Ready," said Osip, his voice even more broken and frightened than that of his brother.

Khabolov turned and looked at the two video machines and the box on top of one of them. The box was filled with tapes. A television set's dead white eye peeked out from behind the machines and tapes.

"Good," said Khabolov, looking at his watch. "I've got to get back to my office. I'll return when I need information or more material. Meanwhile, you prepare a detailed inventory."

"Yes, Comrade," said Felix.

"Yes, Comrade," agreed Osip, who bent to pick up a machine and the box of tapes.

Five minutes later, the load safely locked in the trunk of the car, Khabolov was on his way back to Petrovka. A caseload awaited his careful eye.

"He's gone," sighed Osip from the curtained window as he watched the white Chaika move into traffic and hurry away.

The curtain at the end of the trailer parted and Sasha Tkach stepped out.

"I hope I did it correctly," Sasha said.

"If you did what we showed you, it was fine, fine," whispered Osip, finding a bottle in his drawer and pouring himself a large glass with trembling hands. "It has to be fine. I would rather go to Lubyanka than go through that again."

"I wouldn't," said Felix, reaching for the bottle.

"You did well," said Sasha, "very well."

"You'd like a drink?" Felix asked, turning to the detective with an outstretched hand containing a drink.

"No," said Sasha. It wasn't that he didn't want the drink. Not at all. What he didn't want was the Gorgasali brothers to see that his hands were trembling every bit as much as theirs.

Sarah wasn't home when Rostnikov arrived. He didn't expect her to be. She would be working late, till seven. He would simply go to the second-hand foreign book store on Kachalov Street and wait for her outside. He would smile and tell her that they were going to the circus. She would give him a look that told him she was not going to be able to think about circuses and clowns, that all she could think about was their son, that Josef was in Afghanistan, that madmen were shooting at him, trying to kill him. Her eyes would show that, seek the same fear in his, and he would let the fear show. Then things would be all right. She would nod. They would go to the circus and eat later, afterwards, talking about the acts, about their memories as children. And then she would remember, if she had not by then, the times Porfiry Petrovich had taken the family to the circus. She would remember the little boy's cackling laughter, open-mouthed awe. Then she would weep just a little and they would go to sleep.

There would be no time later to lift his weights. He made himself a plate of cheese, cold meat pie, onions with vinegar, and a slice of bread. There was a half bottle of white wine in the cabinet over the sink. He poured himself a full glass and placed plate and drink on the table near the window, where he could see them while he lifted. Then he changed into his sweatpants and the T-shirt with the words

"Moscow Senior Championship 1983," set out his mat, chair, and weights, and began his routine.

He worked, as always, slowly, deliberately, curling with both hands as he sat, pumping with both hands as he lay on the floor. He was not conscious of the smell of cheese as he began to sweat, but he sensed it. His concentration went to the bar, the weights clanking. He saw nothing, thought nothing. The smell of the food flowed through him as he rolled, moved, lifted, grunted. His T-shirt was soaked through in ten minutes. In twenty minutes his face and neck were itching. He hardly noticed. He was one with the moving weights, the routine. It was at times like this that Rostnikov often lost count, did too much, and only caught himself when his eyes happened to fall on the ticking clock next to his trophy. But this time he did not lose himself. He came out slowly on the last series of repetitions, let himself feel the tension in his stomach as he sat forward with the 150-pound weight behind his back, let himself feel the rivulets of sweat weave their way down his stomach and through the hairs of his crotch. He gave himself a final count, though he knew, could feel, that he was almost finished. He made the sit-ups, eased the weight back to the blanket, and lay back, looking up at the ceiling and the rivers of cracks he could never remember but that came back to him familiarly and clearly each time he was in this position. Rostnikov listened to himself breathe, tightened his stomach, and sat up. The early afternoon light through the window fell on the plate of food and the wineglass, turning them into a still life that pleased Porfiry Petrovich as he put his towel around his neck and lifted himself up awkwardly. The leg was still a bit stiff from Drozhkin's punishment, but it was coming back. A few minutes in the shower and the food would help greatly.

Rostnikov moved slowly still, put the weights back in the cabinet, rolled up the blanket and put it over the weights, and closed the cabinet doors. Then he moved to the bathroom immediately inside the bedroom, stripped off his clothes, examined his dark, solid, and quite hairy body, noticing that even his navel hairs were turning gray, turned on the shower, and waited for the water to turn warm. Hot was too much too expect. Hot had never happened. Warm was a luxury and, as it turned out, a luxury Rostnikov would have to forgo. The water remained cold.

"Yahmm," hummed Rostnikov as he stepped into the stream of cold water, letting it hit his back, his chest, bounce off his head. He took the soap out of the soap box, rubbed himself from head to foot, including his hair, and continued to "Yahmm," pausing only to catch his breath. The soap was a luxury, too—French soap, purchased by Sarah for a price and from a source she preferred not to discuss with her policeman husband. Rostnikov didn't care. He smelled the soap and hummed. Rinsed himself off and hummed. Turned off the water and continued to hum for the few seconds it took to reach the towel. As soon as he touched the towel he stopped humming and thought of his mother at their kitchen table. She smiled, a thin woman with yellow-brown hair, and then the thought was gone.

Rostnikov was brushing his teeth when the phone rang. He wrapped the towel around his ample middle and moved as quickly as he could to the phone in the other room. The phone was both a luxury and a reminder of how near the nearest order was. The phone was his because he was a policeman. The phone was his because sometimes police inspectors had to be reached quickly.

"Rostnikov," he answered, picking up the receiver.

"Karpo," came the familiar voice. "I'm at Elk Island. A row of tree stumps cut for chess players. You know it?"

"I know it," said Rostnikov.

"If you catch a cab, you can get here—"

"In twenty minutes, if I frighten the cabdriver," said Rostnikov, throwing off the towel and reaching for his undershorts as he spoke.

"We may have to move," said Karpo.

Perhaps only Rostnikov would have noticed the very slight change in that monotone, a change so slight that perhaps a dog could not pick it up, but a change he sensed. Rostnikov said nothing. He struggled into his pants as Emil

Karpo added, "I have found the prostitute killer but I cannot arrest him."

Rostnikov tried to buckle his belt with one hand but couldn't.

"He has Mathilde," Karpo said. "And he knows I am here."

"I'm coming," said Rostnikov, and hung up the phone. Although Rostnikov had known about Mathilde Verson for several years, he had finally met her in the hospital a few months ago when Emil Karpo was stubbornly refusing to allow surgery on his arm. She had helped Rostnikov convince the stubborn zealot to agree to let Sarah's cousin Alex perform the operation in his office. Karpo had tried to hide it, but Rostnikov had seen the eyes—not the face, but the eyes—reveal an appreciation, a willingness to respond to the life force of the woman. And now that woman was in the hands of a killer of eight women.

As soon as the phone was down, Rostnikov buckled his pants and put on his shirt. He slipped on his socks, knowing that at least the right one was inside out. The shoes went on without tying. He took four steps to the table, put the cheese and onion on top of the cold meat pie, held the combination in his right hand, and downed the glass of wine with his left. On the way out the door, Rostnikov took his first bite of pie-cheese-meat and found it dry and not nearly as satisfying as he had hoped it would be.

EIGHT

SOMETIME AROUND TWO IN THE AFTERNOON YURI PON had become quite ill, quite ill. It might have been something in the herring he had packed for lunch; the herring did not mix well with the information the computer had given him and then taken away.

"Comrade Pon," Ludmilla Kropetskanoya had said, a slight puckering in the corner of her razor slash of a mouth indicating that she found it distasteful to say what she had to say, "you do not look well."

"I don't feel very well," Pon agreed and let himself feel even worse. He touched his brow and his hand came away moist with sweat.

"I think you have a temperature," she said, reaching over to touch his head. He backed away so quickly he almost fell out of his chair.

"No, don't," he squealed. She had never touched him. The idea of her touching him with those cold steel fingers made him retch.

"I'm . . ." she began and then shook her head. "Go home. You're sick. Fill out your sheet and go home. Things are slow. We have the extra help. Go take care of

yourself. You've been behaving, I have to say this, like a
man about to fly to the moon."

"How does a man who is about to fly to the moon feel?"
he said, looking down to hide the hatred he was feeling
toward her.

"Frightened," she said calmly.

"I wouldn't be afraid to go to the moon," he said, looking up at her defiantly. "I would not be afraid to go to the
moon."

This look on her face was a new one, one he had never
seen before, and it frightened Yuri Pon. Ludmilla's eyes
opened wide and her mouth went slack as she looked at
him. Then the tight rubber face returned to near-normal. It
had been a look of surprise, possibly even fear.

"I'm sorry," Yuri said, touching his own forehead. "I
must be feverish, a bit feverish. I've been working hard on
the computer. It's—"

"Go home," she said. "Now. Go home and take care of
yourself. That is an order, Comrade."

Orders, he thought. This woman gives orders. I could
give her orders. I could get my briefcase, get my knife.
Then I would give the orders. But he knew he would do no
such thing. The knife wasn't for withered goat tails like
Ludmilla. It was for young, filthy women. On Ludmilla he
would have to use something that didn't bring him close to
her, didn't force him to touch or smell her. A club, a chair.
He thought of the statue of a Greek goddess in his mother's
room, a cheap copy his mother had purchased at a market,
a cheap replica with a small chip in the base. He could
bring that down on Ludmilla's face again and again and
again.

Yuri forced himself to stand up. It was difficult. He
tried not to tremble with rage, confusion, and that aching,
longing feeling.

"Home, now," Ludmilla repeated. "If you still feel like
this tomorrow, you go to the clinic and have them look at
you and fill out a report."

"Yes, Comrade," he whispered. "Thank you. I do
feel . . ."

She had already turned her back and was marching toward a uniformed officer at the desk. Yuri shut his mouth and moved to the small closet near the door where he kept his jacket and briefcase. Behind him he heard Ludmilla take a file from the officer, heard them speak, but he could not make out the words. As soon as Yuri's fingers touched the handle of his briefcase, he found it difficult to breathe. He needed air, desperately needed air. He took in large gulps of air and looked back over his shoulder at Ludmilla, who continued to talk to the officer but looked at her departing assistant as if he were a disfigured beggar.

Yuri didn't stop to make out an early departure report. He knew he would never make it if he did. As it was, he barely got to the main entrance, where the uniformed and armed guard on duty watched him emotionlessly as he puffed and grunted to the door and out into the afternoon sun. Two men and a woman he recognized from the Procurator's Office moved past him, eyeing him as he gulped in air and loosened his tie. An efficient-looking woman in a dark suit whom he didn't know asked him if he needed help. Yuri couldn't speak, but he shook his head no and stumbled down the steps into the square. He looked across the street toward the stern statue of Felix Dzerzhinsky.

He stumbled across Kirov Street and was almost hit by a Volga whose driver leaned out the window and shouted something at him before speeding on. The steps of the Dzerzhinsky Metro Station were in front of him. He went to the rail and looked down into the darkness of the station and decided that he could not go down there, not now. A family—five or six people, probably foreign—was coming out of the Mayakovsky Museum to his left. They were talking loudly, arguing about something. They headed toward the metro, and Yuri clutched his briefcase and stumbled away, crossing Serov Passage, managing to avoid traffic. He began to walk aimlessly down the street. At the entrance to the museum, Yuri stopped, adjusted his glasses, and looked around as if he were lost. Then he turned around, headed back to the square, looked up at the sun, and crossed New Square Street in front of the Detsky

Mir children's shop. He passed the store entrance and moved up 25th October Street.

Yuri was in the wrong area for what he needed, wanted. His moist fingers tightened on the worn handle of the briefcase as he wandered. He looked only forward, not back, and had he looked back in his present state it was doubtful that he would have seen the tall, gaunt man and the woman in the red hat who were following him.

"He's sick," said Mathilde, hurrying to keep pace with Karpo.

"Yes," agreed Emil Karpo, following Pon through the afternoon crowd, trying to stay far enough back to keep from being seen. Karpo was well aware that he did not melt well into a crowd. Mathilde's new red hat did not add to the possibility of their successfully blending into the pedestrian traffic, but Pon was not a man to notice. He had stumbled out of Petrovka, and they followed him simply because he was the first of the three possible suspects to leave that day. They would have pursued any of the three who came out first. The plan would have been the same in any case.

They had, however, almost missed Pon. One of the suspects was an investigating officer who might come out any time on assignment. Pon was an office worker. It was hours earlier than his normal departure time.

"I don't like the way he looks," said Mathilde as they walked.

Karpo shrugged. He didn't care how Pon looked as he staggered around the streets of Moscow.

"Do you think it's him?" Mathilde asked. Pon stopped suddenly, clutched his briefcase to his chest, and looked across the street toward the elevated parkway where the statue of Ivan Fyodorov, the first Russian printer, stood. Karpo put out a hand to halt Mathilde.

"Wait," he said.

Pon seemed to be about to cross the street, changed his mind, and continued walking. Across from the Slavyansky Bazaar Restaurant five minutes later, Pon adjusted his slip-

ping glasses once more and turned his head back toward
Karpo and Mathilde. Mathilde was about to stop but Karpo
reached out, grabbed her hand, and kept walking behind a
young couple.

"Don't stop. If we stop, we stand out," he said. "If he
doesn't start walking again, we turn in to the first doorway."

But Yuri Pon did decide to walk again. He walked and
walked. For almost an hour he wandered almost aimlessly,
and as he walked he sweated, and as he sweated he began
to recover a bit from whatever was ailing him.

"I'm tired," sighed Mathilde.

Karpo looked at Pon, who had paused in front of the
Cosmos Hotel and moved toward the entrance. The
Cosmos lobby was not exactly the place where one might
encounter a prostitute, but Mathilde was tiring and Pon
showed no signs of ceasing his wandering.

"Now, in the lobby," Karpo said.

"Aren't you going to tell me to be careful?" she asked
playfully.

Karpo looked down at her, at the thin layer of perspiration on her slightly protruding upper lip.

"I don't believe my telling you to be careful would
make you more cautious. You are already aware of the
danger," he said.

Pon had gone through the hotel doors and disappeared.

"That's true," said Mathilde, shaking her head. "I
thought of it more as a sign of . . . forget it. Good-bye. Stay
close behind."

"As close as I safely can," he said.

He watched her hurry to the hotel, holding her hat down
on her head as she moved. He paused as she entered the
lobby and then followed her, moving at a normal pace.

Yuri Pon was not sure how he had wandered into the
hotel lobby. People bustled around him, his glasses threatened to slip off his nose, the briefcase felt heavy and hurt
his arm. He shifted it to the other hand and realized that he
was sweating, almost drenched.

And then the feeling came over him as it had in Petrovka. He was inside. He could not breathe. He had to get out, stay out, perhaps he would never be able to go indoors again. He almost ran into the woman as he backed away and turned toward the hotel doors.

"Careful," said the woman in the red hat and dress, reaching out to keep him from falling.

"I'm, I'm . . . I have to get outside. I don't feel so well," he said, hurrying past her onto the street. That was better. Oh, it was much better.

"Are you sure you're all right?" the woman in the hat said behind him. She had followed him out. He stepped out of the way of a soldier in uniform, an officer who marched quickly into the hotel.

"I'm better," Yuri Pon said.

The woman took his arm to help him. His first impulse was to shrug her off, but she was not Ludmilla. This was a younger woman, a pretty woman with a nice smell.

"I'll help you," she said, and he let her help him.

"It's all right," he said after a few seconds of standing at the curb. "It's hot."

"Yes," the woman in red said. "It's hot. You look like a prosperous businessman?"

"I'm a file cle—, a files supervisor in the Central Petrovka Station," he said.

"I think you should lie down somewhere," the woman said. "I know a place not far away where we could go. You could rest, lie down, perhaps even enjoy yourself a bit. Just a short taxi drive away."

Yuri Pon turned his eyes toward the woman and looked at her seriously for the first time. She was pretty, or close to pretty, and she was a prostitute. He had stumbled upon her. The excitement welled within him. He jiggled the briefcase and laughed.

The woman backed away for an instant, her eyes opening in puzzlement, and then she returned to his arm.

"What's so funny?" she said. "I like to share a joke with a man."

"I was looking for you," he said.

"Magic." The woman sighed. "Fate brought us together. Do we find a taxi?"

"No taxi," Pon said, taking her hand. "No taxi. Taxis are too . . ."

"Constricting?" Mathilde said.

"Yes," Yuri agreed. "No taxi."

He suddenly took her right hand and began pulling her with him down the street.

"What—?" she began.

"Hurry!" Yuri cried. "We'll miss it."

At the corner a trolleybus stood, its door starting to close. They got to it just in time to reach in and grab the door. He pulled the woman onto the bus, paid the eight kopecks for the two of them, and dragged her to an open pair of seats as the bus pulled away.

"What is—?" the woman began.

"Wait . . . wait," Pon said, pushing his glasses onto his nose with his palm. He let go of her hand and clutched the briefcase to his chest. Two uniformed sailors looked at the woman and Pon and whispered to each other.

"Yes, yes, it's all right," Pon said with a smile. "I can breathe."

"Good," the woman said with her own smile, looking toward the back of the bus. Yuri looked back, too. There was no one there.

"Where are we going?" she asked him in a whisper.

"The park," he said. "I want to take you to the park."

Emil Karpo walked up to the two cabdrivers in front of the Cosmos Hotel. Both drivers wore little caps. The smaller of the two wore a long-sleeved gray shirt with the sleeves rolled up unevenly. He had hairy arms; the hair was reddish brown. The second driver was bigger, heavier, louder.

"So you put up relatives if you think it's so easy, Comrade Smart Guy," the heavy cabbie shouted, sweat speckling his brow. "I'm lucky I've got a bedroom. But you can't turn away a sister's family. I ask you."

"And I answer you," said the smaller one. "If I had

relatives from Kiev, I'd take them in till we were sure."

"Easy for you to say," the big man said, grunting, noticing the pale man advancing toward them. "Everyone in your family is from Moscow."

"No. My cousin Alexei is in Brezhnev. . ."

The gaunt man was standing next to them now, not as tall or heavy as the big cab driver, but impossible to ignore.

"Whose cab is that?" Karpo said.

"Mine," said the smaller driver.

"Get in," said Karpo.

"I'm talking to my friend," the little man with the hairy arms said with irritation.

Karpo's left arm shot out and grasped the small driver's arm.

"Get in, now."

The bigger driver reached out and grabbed Karpo's wrist.

"Let him go, you zombie," he hissed.

Karpo released the hairy arm, snapped his hand down suddenly, and whipped his fingers up to the moist, thick neck of the big driver. The long fingers tightened and the big man gagged and lost his hat. A small crowd had begun to gather, to watch, to do nothing.

"Into the cab," Karpo said without looking at the smaller driver, who hurried into his car. The long fingers opened and the red-faced cabbie staggered back into a white-haired man with a briefcase.

Without looking back, Karpo got into the cab, closed the door, and said, "That bus. Follow it."

The short driver didn't even nod. He started the cab and drove in silence.

Thirty minutes later, after dozens of stops and starts, in the northeastern section of the city just at the Outer Ring Road, a heavy, sweating man carrying a briefcase and a woman in red with a red hat got off a bus. The sweating man looked back at the rows of apartments to his right and then over at the vast wooded area to his left.

"Here," said Karpo.

"Losiny Ostrov, Elk Island," said the cab driver.

"I know where I am," Karpo said, getting out of the cab and handing the cabbie a five-ruble bill.

The cabbie hesitated; he had been given either too little or too much money, but he decided not to speak to the man who was standing on the curb next to the cab. Instead, the cabbie threw the car into first gear, made a sudden U-turn in front of a truck, and sped away.

Karpo crossed the street behind the bus, walking slowly, keeping Pon and Mathilde in sight but not too close. His plan was to move in on Pon, frighten him into a confession or a slip. Hard evidence would not be essential. The courts would accept slips of the tongue, mistakes, a forced search of Pon's home for evidence. Karpo needed little more and he was confident that he was about to get what he needed. Pon was walking like a penguin, sweating like a man who had just run a marathon in hundred-degree heat. In one hand he held his briefcase. In the other he held the wrist of Mathilde.

"I was born not fifteen miles from here," Pon said to the woman in the red hat. "Mytishy. My mother still lives there. Right over there. Beyond the woods."

He pointed, and her eyes pretended to follow.

"And over there," Pon said, pointing in another direction as he led her into the park, "is Kalingrad and Bala-shikha."

"You are hurting my arm," Mathilde said calmly as they passed an old man with a large belly. The old man was wearing shorts and a yellow shirt. He glanced at them and walked on, minding his own business.

Pon ignored Mathilde and led her on, his voice growing more excited with each step. His grip tightened as they stopped in front of long, neat rows of birches on both sides of the path leading into the park.

"When I was a boy," Pon said, panting, "this was still just called a forest. Now it's a national park, a national park. Look at that sign."

He nodded at a tall wooden sign marking the entrance of

the park. A small round picture of an elk's head hovered over the embossed number 1406.

"I know all about this park, all about it," Pon said, hardly noticing the woman he was pulling along. "I spent my days in here, in the darkness of the trees, alone. A fat, smelly boy alone. I wasn't sorry for myself. No, no, no. I wasn't. I liked it here. That sign. In 1406 the name Losiny Ostrov was first mentioned in a will left by a prince of Muscovy. There are tales," he suddenly whispered, leaning toward her ear, "tales of the sinful things that the prince did in these woods to young women. Would you like to hear these tales?"

"No," Mathilde said, looking back over her shoulder.

"No," mocked Yuri Pon. "No. You have tales every bit as terrible. You think you do, but you don't. I have a secret for you. Shh. I'll share it up ahead in my favorite place, near the river."

He pulled her ahead along the path, past people sitting on benches, deeper into the woods. Mathilde could hear the splash of water, the voices of children at play.

"Before 1406, as early as 1388, this area was recorded under another name in certain documents," Pon went on. He was beginning to give off a terrible odor, the smell of sweat and possibly something worse. Mathilde wanted to pull herself away, to run, but his grip was surprisingly strong.

"No dogs allowed in this park," Pon said, lurching along the path without looking at her. "No dogs. There are more than a hundred and sixty species of birds. Some of them build their nests on the ground. They have enough natural enemies without bringing dogs in here. At night, the bird calls are marvelous. Peter the First, sometime after 1670, made this the first state forest in all of Russia in which it was prohibited to fell trees except those that were dead or damaged by disease or fire. This is a clean park. Moscow was a clean city. Elk are all over. Even wild boars. Wait, wait, I must take you to the giant pine that slants, the Tower of Pisa."

He dragged her past three young men sitting on tree

stumps. Two of the young men were playing chess on another tree stump. All three men wore glasses. None of
them looked up at the woman in red and the sweating man
who dragged her to a bench.

It was at this point that Karpo, keeping Pon and Mathilde in sight, managed to call Rostnikov from a public
phone in the clearing. He called because Yuri Pon, as he
sat on the bench and pulled Mathilde down next to him,
looked directly at Karpo through his thick-lensed glasses,
opened his briefcase with one hand, and extracted a long-
bladed knife that caught the late afternoon sunlight.

A jogger crossed the path in front of Karpo, who kept
his unblinking eyes on Pon and Mathilde. Pon, in turn,
placed his briefcase on his lap to hide the knife and held
tightly to Mathilde's wrist. His eyes began to blink like
those of a diseased owl. His glasses refused to remain on
his moist nose, and he had to keep pushing them back on
by twitching his nose and throwing back his head. Karpo
walked slowly to the bench facing Pon across the path.
They were, perhaps, a dozen feet away from each other.
People passed between them, and Mathilde fixed Karpo
with an angry glare. He did not look at her. They sat silently for fifteen or twenty minutes while people moved
past in both directions and the sounds of people, and even
of an occasional animal in the woods, rustled through the
pines and grass.

"I have a philosophy," Pon finally called to Karpo after
a family of picnickers had argued their way past the
benches. "You want to hear it?"

Karpo said nothing.

"All right, then," Pon said. "I'll tell you anyway. There
is a bit of animal in each of us. We are born with it. We
are, as our history and biology books tell us, all animals.
And what is an animal?"

Karpo remained silent, unblinking.

"An animal thinks only of its immediate gratification.
Food, sex, or the blind preservation of its species," Pon
explained. "It is natural."

Pon paused to watch a young girl walk past. His head

turned to follow her. His mouth opened as if he could not breathe and then his eyes returned to Karpo.

"It is natural," Pon went on, picking up his thought. "But we are civilized. We are taught that machines are more functional than animals. Machines do not feel. They perform without feeling, without thought. We are taught to be machines. You see the contradiction? We are caught between being animals and being machines. It can drive us mad. We live balanced, don't you see? When they say someone has become unbalanced, that is what they mean, that he has fallen into his animalism or given up his humanity to become a machine."

"And what has that to do with you?" Mathilde said calmly and so quietly that Karpo barely heard her over the sounds of shouting swimmers somewhere beyond the trees.

"I have channeled my animalism into a useful social function," Pon explained, still looking at Karpo. "I respond to my animalism and rid the state of criminals it cannot allow itself to acknowledge. Prostitutes, like you."

Pon held Mathilde's hand up high. The briefcase slipped from his lap and the knife was naked in his lap. Four old men and an old woman appeared around a bend in the path and headed their way.

"I suggest," said Karpo calmly, "that you hide your knife."

Pon put the knife behind his back and pressed Mathilde's hand into his lap. As the five old people passed by, Pon rubbed Mathilde's hand between his legs.

"The animal," Pon mouthed to Karpo soundlessly.

The old people were about twenty feet down the path when Pon pulled the knife out from behind his back. For some reason, the old woman at the rear of the quintet picked that moment to glance back, and she saw the sweating man on the bench holding a knife, saw the woman in the red dress try to pull away, saw the man who looked like a ghost rise and move forward. The old woman was quite sure that the ghost would not cross the path before the man with the knife plunged it into the young woman. The old woman wanted to turn away from the sight, away from her helplessness, away from her own memories of a war long ago and her uncle lying dead with bayonet wounds forming red-black exclamation marks in his side.

The four old men walked on but the old woman stood, watched, waited for the knife to come down, but it didn't. Then, suddenly, a barrel of a man crashed through the thick trees behind the bench of the sweating owl with the knife. The barrel-shaped man caught the wrist of the owl, wrenched the man's hand from the wrist of the woman, and pulled suddenly upward. The sweating man, the heavy sweating man, rose from the bench, a look of surprise on his face, his glasses dropping to the path. The barrel-shaped man stepped back and gave a mighty pull, and the sweating man went bouncing backward over the bench with a terrible release of air as he hit the ground, as the ghostly man leaped over the bench.

"No!" screamed the sweating man, trying to rise.

"Yes," said the ghostly man, kicking the knife out of his hand.

The woman in red stood safely on the path side of the bench, clutching her red hat in her hands.

"Olga," croaked one of the old men far down the path, "what are you doing?"

For an instant the old woman was bewildered. No one was dead. She did not know what was happening, what had happened or why, but no one was dead. The woman in red looked at Olga and smiled, and Olga Korechakova, who had not felt like smiling in at least two decades, smiled back and turned to join the old men in the park.

NINE

"**I** DON'T WANT TO GO TO THE CIRCUS."

Sarah Rostnikov was more weary and distracted than emphatic. Rostnikov had been waiting for her outside the second-hand foreign book store where she worked on Kachalov Street. He had gone home to change into his favorite comfortable pants, worn shiny in the rear and the knees, and his favorite gray turtleneck sweater. In contrast, Sarah wore a black suit and white blouse. She had not been expecting him. She was not dressed for a circus. She had looked forward to a quick ride back to the apartment, a bath—even if she had to cart kettles of boiled water, which she usually had to do—a simple meal of whatever was left over, and a quiet evening listening to music on the radio.

"You will enjoy the circus," Rostnikov said, taking her arm.

"The circus is noisy. It smells of animals. It will take us an hour to get home when it's over. I'm hungry. I'm tired," she said to the night breeze.

"We'll stop at a *stolovaya* for some *kotleta* and potatoes with a little kvass," he said, leading her through the early evening crowd. "We'll call it a celebration. I have free passes."

"Porfiry Petrovich," Sarah said, stopping suddenly, "what have we to celebrate? Josef is being shot at by barbarians. You have been demoted. The KGB has us on some kind of list for troublemakers. What have we to celebrate?"

People moved around them, and Rostnikov shifted his weight to his good leg and touched the red hair of his wife.

"Work, health, appetites, and curiosity," he said.

"You are an optimist, Rostnikov," Sarah said with a smile and a shake of her head.

"I'm a Muscovite," he answered. "And I have a passion for the circus."

"And for cabbage soup and meat pies," she sighed.

They had eaten quietly at a luncheonette near the circus. Rostnikov had consumed three meat pies, a bowl of cabbage soup, and quantities of bread and double potatoes. Sarah had a bowl of cabbage soup, which she didn't quite finish.

"What was your day like?" he said after he had finished the final crumb of bread, which he dipped into the final touch of sauce from the pasty.

"I sold books," Sarah said with a shrug, pushing away her soup. "The party representative for the store gave a lunchtime lecture on productivity and how it was our duty to sell more Bulgarian books on breeding goats. What did you do?"

"I helped Emil Karpo catch a man who had murdered eight prostitutes," he said.

She looked at him and at the young couple hovering nearby who obviously wanted their table now that they had finished their meal.

"Good," said Sarah. "You should have shot him."

"He is quite mad."

"That is of little solace to the women he killed," she said.

"You should be a judge," Rostnikov said, standing awkwardly to protect his leg.

"And you should be a plumber," Sarah replied.

"I am a plumber," Rostnikov said, leading her past the waiting couple, who pounced on the now-empty table.

Twenty minutes later they joined the crowds under the neon sign of the New Circus. They were shown to their seats, very good seats, in the second row.

"Why do I know this is not simply a night at the circus?" Sarah whispered.

Rostnikov sighed and looked at her. "We came at the invitation of a killer. I could not bring myself to disappoint him."

"I see," said Sarah. "And why was it necessary that I come?"

"Because," said Rostnikov quietly as the lights went down, "I need you."

"To do what?"

"To be with me," he said as the music blared forth in a rush of brass and Dimitri Mazaraki stepped out to the center of the ring, huge, confident, giving his fine mustache a twirl of conceit. He was dressed in red—a red coat, red pants, even a red top hat. The music stopped, and the big announcer's eyes, scanning the audience with a Cheshire grin, silencing one and all—men, women, and children—silenced them with the secret he held of magic to be performed, mystery to be savored, danger to be witnessed, fantasy to store for the gray day tomorrow.

Mazaraki's eyes played over the crowd, roamed beyond the silence, and snapped onto Rostnikov right in front of him in the second row. Mazaraki's smile changed, the lip curled ever so slightly below the fine mustache. Rostnikov replied with a smile of his own, a sad smile that caused the announcer's lip to hesitate for only a moment before he turned his eyes back to the crowd and announced the first act.

The music came blaring forth again. Mazaraki stepped back into the shadows, and a dancing bear and two mandolin players dressed in plaid suits and baggy pants bounded into the ring.

"That was your killer?" asked Sarah, leaning toward her husband.

Rostnikov nodded.

He felt her grip tighten on his arm.

Emil Karpo sat at his desk on the fifth floor of Petrovka finishing his report. He had no office and his desk was number five in a line of eleven desks against a windowless wall. The windows were all in the offices on the outer wall. An officer named Fyodor sat at desk number nine talking on the telephone. Karpo could make out nothing that Fyodor said. He didn't care. But he could not ignore the snorting laugh that usually followed a deep intake of air by the other inspector.

He finished the report and looked over at the only other person in the office.

"It's almost nine," Mathilde said, playing with her wilted red hat. She seemed generally wilted. Her hair lay across her cheeks. The collar on one side of her red dress was up, the other down, and it was clear that this lack of symmetry was not a clever fashion ploy.

"It is finished," said Karpo. "I need only make copies and carry them to the deputy procurator's office."

"And then?"

"And then," said Karpo, rising, "you are free to go."

Mathilde put the hat over her face and laughed. It was a loud, rough laugh that rivaled that of Fyodor, who paused in his conversation with a smile and looked over at the woman in red to share her joke. When Fyodor saw Karpo looking back at him, however, he returned to his phone conversation.

"Something is humorous?" Karpo asked, standing in front of Mathilde, the report, in duplicate, on Yuri Pon neatly tucked into a folder under his left arm.

"I was almost killed this afternoon," Mathilde said, choking back a hiccup. "That madman almost killed me."

"I was there," Karpo said reasonably.

"Oh, yes, of course. How could I have forgotten?"

"I did not literally mean—" Karpo began.

"No, you did not literally mean," she said, standing. "You literally are. Do you know that I was frightened this afternoon? Do you think it might be reasonable to offer me something? Thanks, an arm of support, an American tap on the chin for a job well done?"

"The hat . . ." Karpo said.

"With the money I could have made picking up Englishmen at the Bolshoi today, I could have bought five hats," she said, putting the hat on the chair.

"Well?"

"Well? Is that what you have to say? It's your turn to speak, Emil Karpo. Your turn."

Her hands were on her hips. A moist clump of hair fell over her eyes. She tried to blow it away but it didn't move. She flicked it over with her fingertips.

"You helped to catch a man who committed eight murders of women," he said evenly. "You seemed quite willing to—"

"*Spasee'ba*, thank you," she said.

"*Spasee'ba*," Karpo said. "On behalf of the people of Moscow."

"I'm touched," she said with a sigh, picking up her hat again. "You are a romantic, Emil Karpo."

"I don't see how you could come to such a conclusion," he said. "Certainly not based on the information you have or on anything I have said or done here."

Fyodor laughed, and both Mathilde and Karpo turned to see if he were laughing at them. He was not.

"I was being sarcastic, Emil."

"As you well know, I have no sense of humor," Karpo said soberly. "I have no repressions and, therefore, no need for humor."

"Do you know what day it is?" she asked.

"Tuesday," he replied.

A door somewhere opened and closed, the sound echoing past them.

"Let us break the pattern," she whispered and found herself unable to repress a hiccup. "Let us go to your apartment, which I have never seen, and let us get in bed."

"It isn't Thursday," Karpo said.

"Believe me," she replied. "It will still work."

"Why do you want to do this?" he asked with genuine curiosity.

"Why? Because you are a challenge to my profession, to my craft. I am driven to make you feel, to make you react."

Karpo shook his head, unable to understand this woman.

"And I am to pay as always?" he asked.

"Yes," she said, plunking the red hat on her head. "You are to pay as always. The hat was for risking my life."

"I see," he said. "Compensation for lost income. And you don't want cash without expending labor."

"I love when you talk filthy to me," she said with a grin.

"I didn't . . ."

"Deliver your report and let's go," she said. "While I still labor under the delusion that there is hope for you."

The circus crowd responded with enthusiastic applause to the panorama display of the fighting spirit of the Red Army. A woman stood upon a great horse that pranced around the ring. The woman held high a red flag with the hammer and sickle. In the darkness beyond the curtain, a cannon roared. Twelve men dressed as soldiers high-stepped out and raised their rifles to the sky in salute. The applause rose again.

Rostnikov noted that the applause came nowhere near matching that which had been given to the trick horse rider or the dancing bear or the clown on the high wire or any other act before this one.

Throughout the evening, Mazaraki had moved closer to the crowd with each announcement of each act, had moved closer and closer to Rostnikov.

"For the benefit of our foreign visitors," Mazaraki had said, looking at Rostnikov during his introduction of a motorcycle act, "the New Moscow Circus does not promote the idea of danger in its performance. Skill is the focus, Soviet skills. Our people come, not in the hope of witnessing accident or death, but with confidence that they will see performers who have perfected their skills, their timing, and the potential with which they have been born and that our nation has nurtured. And yet, Tovarich," he said, looking directly at Rostnikov with a grin, "some skills have a risk of danger, and those who come through the doors of the circus must understand that there is always the slight possibility of accident for those who would challenge their skills, their muscles, their wit. There is no better place than the circus for such a challenge."

"He's talking to you," Sarah whispered.

Rostnikov said nothing. He watched the announcer in red describe the motorcycle act, watched him back away, watched the look in the man's eyes, which he had seen many times before during investigations—a look of defiance and desperation.

The last act before the curtain call by all the performers was a magician, a magnificent magician with two bespangled women assistants whom he kept making disappear and reappear in various sections of the audience, high above on a rafter, or inside one of the four locked boxes on a raised platform.

Children clapped, men and women said "wonderful," and the performers and animals made a final triumphant appearance. As the performers left and the final strains of a march vibrated from the band, Rostnikov looked at the exit curtain, looked at Dimitri Mazaraki looking back at him. The tickets had been the first invitation. All night long, throughout the performance, Mazaraki had issued other invitations. And now came the last, a look that said "Come if you dare, but I doubt if you dare, not in my world."

It was, Rostnikov thought, the bear trapped in a shed, standing on its hind legs, growling, claws up, paws wavering, a frightening and frightened figure.

"Take the metro home," Rostnikov said to his wife as the crowd began to thin and the band stopped playing. "I'll be there as soon as I can."

Sarah looked at him and avoided a sticky, crying little boy who was being led out by his mother.

"What are you doing, Porfiry Petrovich?"

She was tired, worried, and well aware that she had no chance of changing his mind regardless of what he was going to do.

"Delivering a message," he said. "From a man who sat on Gogol's head."

"I'm staying," she said firmly.

"If you stay, I will worry about you," he told her gently. "If I worry, I cannot do what I must do."

There were only a few people left in the arena now. Sarah Rostnikov looked around and back at her husband.

"You didn't plan this?"

"No," he said, shaking his head. "I thought I had another day."

"And . . ."

"Another day may be too late."

The voices of the stragglers, the sounds of their feet shuffling tired on the concrete steps, dropped another level. There was nothing more to say. Sarah touched her husband's arm, turned her back, and walked slowly after the others.

TEN

Rostnikov waited till the entire arena was clear and then he turned, walked down three steps, and sat in the same seat in which he had sat for the entire performance. Five minutes later a squad of cleaning women in babushkas came out. They came through the main curtain like a new act, the jabbering cleaning women. Rostnikov watched them divide into duets and climb into the seats with their arsenals of brooms, rags, bags, and pans.

The two who had his section noticed Rostnikov later than they would have had he betrayed his presence with any movement, but notice him they did.

"Show is over," said the older and heavier of the two *babushkas*.

"Not yet," said Rostnikov, his eyes not on her but on the entrance curtain.

"We've got to clean up," she said with one hand on her hip and the other using her broom to point to the rows of stands.

Rostnikov shifted slightly to remove his identity card. He held it up to the woman without looking at her. The other cleaning woman, a shorter version of the leader, leaned forward to look at the card.

"We'll clean around him," the older woman announced, and they went about their business. In less than twenty minutes the women had finished their cleaning act and exited as they had come. Some of the women turned their heads to look at the bulky man sitting alone in the arena. The older *babushka* who had seen his identification card spoke to a woman at her side as they departed, and more heads turned to look at him. Then they were gone and all that remained was the overhead humming of the lights. Suddenly the lights began to click off. There was a pattern. The lights behind Rostnikov went off first and then, like a row of dominoes, the other lights clicked off in a wave until the only illumination in the circus arena came from a quartet of night lights mounted on the floor. They cast a dull glow in the circle in front of Rostnikov as if waiting for a final, ghostly performance.

And still Rostnikov sat. He thought, after another five minutes or so, that he heard something in the darkness beyond the lights. The direction was uncertain. He sat almost certain that he was now being watched. He wanted to shift his leg to keep it from going stiff but he did not move. Another sound. In front? Above?

"The next performance isn't until tomorrow." Mazaraki's voice came from the darkness.

Rostnikov said nothing, did not try to find the man behind the voice.

Mazaraki laughed. The laughter echoed in the dark circle of the arena like the screams of a dozen madmen.

"You are in my world, policeman," Mazaraki said. Rostnikov thought the voice had moved. Yes, to the right in front of him and possibly above. No, definitely above.

"I am going to guess something, policeman. I'm going to guess that you have told no one else what you suspect. Am I right? I'm right. And now, policeman, you are trapped in the light like a fish in a tank."

Rostnikov was certain now where the voice was coming from. He turned his head upward and fixed his eyes directly on the point in the shadows where Mazaraki must be standing. "It is you who stand naked in the light, Dimitri Mazaraki."

From the darkness came the shuffling, slipping sound of Mazaraki taking a step backward.

Rostnikov stood up then and walked down two steps, ignoring the electric tingling in his leg. He walked to the center of the circle and beyond. Above him Mazaraki scrambled heavily, his footsteps echoing on metal. Rostnikov reached the far side of the circle and moved to one of the four lights that were fixed on the center of the arena. He reached down and with both hands pulled the metal light fixture. It was reluctant to move, but he forced it upward, upward. It was like a cannonball, a single a dumbbell heavier than any he had attempted before. It fought him for seconds and then gave up.

Above him Mazaraki continued to scramble. Rostnikov turned in front of the beam and looked upward. His own huge shadow was cast over the seats—a faint, broad shadow—and just above the head of the shadow the faint light found Mazaraki, one foot on the rope ladder leading down from the high wire. Mazaraki, still clad in his red suit, looked down over his shoulder. His hat slipped from his head and floated like a bird in slow motion downward toward Rostnikov, who watched it land, bounce, roll in a circle, and stop.

"I'm coming, policeman," Mazaraki said.

"I'm here," replied Rostnikov as Mazaraki climbed down in the shadow of the policeman.

Mazaraki came steadily, without panting, without effort. Rostnikov was fascinated by the grace of the huge body and the pose the man in red took when he reached the ground. Mazaraki stood for an instant with his hands on his hips. There was a smile below his mustache. He took a dozen steps forward and beckoned for Rostnikov to meet him. Rostnikov made no reply in word or movement. His gray shadow now covered the hatless announcer, who took the final ten steps and stood in front of Rostnikov. Mazaraki was at least six inches taller. The big man's right hand came out and grasped Rostnikov's left arm above the elbow. The wool of the gray sweater scratched Rostnikov's arm. The eyes of the two men met, and Rostnikov reached over with his right hand, got a firm grip on Mazaraki's thick, hairy wrist, and began to squeeze slowly.

"The game will soon end," whispered Mazaraki. "Your moment in the ring will be over. I will crush your head and throw your body in the park."

The smile on Mazaraki's face was fixed, his teeth remarkably white and even, the teeth of a performer, but beads of sweat were forming on the big man's brow and his cheeks. Rostnikov's left arm was beginning to go numb where Mazaraki squeezed. The light Rostnikov had turned upward now hit the big man's face, casting the upward shadows Josef used to make with a lamp: the scary face, the dark eye sockets, the black mouth.

And then Mazaraki's dark smile contorted suddenly. He gasped, let go of Rostnikov's arm, and tried to pull his hand back, but Rostnikov didn't let it go. Mazaraki struggled to free himself, jerked back to make the smaller man release him, but Rostnikov didn't budge. His grip was like a metal spring trap on Mazaraki's wrist. Mazaraki lashed out with his left fist, a thundering hammer of a blow. Rostnikov stepped forward, leaned over, and rammed his head into Mazaraki's exposed stomach just below the blow, which barely touched the top of Rostnikov's head.

A *wooof* sound escaped from Mazaraki, and Rostnikov released his wrist. The announcer in red fell on his rear into the center of the circle. He writhed on the ground, got to his knees holding his stomach, groaned, and slowly stood.

"I'm not going to jail," Mazaraki shouted defiantly, one hand on his stomach.

"I'm not taking you to jail," Rostnikov replied.

Mazaraki's new mask was one of puzzlement.

"You lie." He laughed, and his laughter once again echoed through the arena.

"Why would I lie?" Rostnikov said.

"I killed Pesknoko," Mazaraki said. "And Duznetzov.

He killed himself because he was afraid, afraid of what would be done to him because he was weak, because he might talk. Do you know what he might talk about?"

"You were smuggling people across the borders to the West," Rostnikov said as Mazaraki tried to straighten up, pull himself together for another frantic attack.

"Yes, but how did you . . . ?" Mazaraki said, and then got an idea. He looked up at Rostnikov with a new understanding. "Yes," he said again, "I see. You're not going to put me in jail. You haven't told anyone. You want me to get you out. You, and some family members. A wife? Daughter? Huh? Ha. Now it is clear."

Rostnikov said nothing. He held his ground. But something had hit him low in the stomach. The voice of a warlock was speaking to him.

"It can be done," Mazaraki said in a whisper of conspiracy that would have been heard by anyone who happened to be in the darkness of the arena. "You take a vacation, say you are going to the mountains or Yalta, but you come with the troupe. We are about to go on tour. You come with the group to Lithuania. I have false papers so you can even cross the border into Poland. And in Poland I know people who can get you into Germany, West Germany. It can be done, policeman. I've done it dozens of times."

Nausea. Rostnikov felt nausea as he imagined for an instant himself, Sarah, Josef, each carrying a suitcase, climbing into a car with someone who spoke with a Polish accent.

"Katya Rashkovskaya," Rostnikov said, to pull himself away from the temptation of the image. "You tried to kill her."

"Of course," said Mazaraki through clenched teeth, fighting off the last of the first shock of pain. "If I don't kill her, she will kill me."

"Kill you?" Rostnikov said as Mazaraki stood almost upright.

"Whose idea do you think all of this was?" Mazaraki said with a shake of his head. "I never thought about smuggling people, doing anything but some black marketing of a few radios from France. It was her idea when they joined the circus. She kept Pesknoko in line, Duznetzov. And then when Duznetzov weakened and said he could take no more she got me to threaten him. She decided that we had to get rid of Pesknoko. Then, only then, did I realize that she would have to kill me, have to get rid of me, or I might drag her down if I got caught. Don't you see? Don't you understand?"

"It makes—" Rostnikov began.

But Mazaraki hulked forward and cut in, "I only tried to kill her to protect myself. You are a joke, policeman. You've done all this to protect the woman but she is the one you want. You are a joke but we can turn the joke. We can both get her and I can get you and your family into the West. You're thinking about it."

His voice was now a soothing whisper.

"I saw that look in your eyes. I've seen it before in the eyes of black marketers, government bureaucrats, scientists, and even a KGB man. I can get you out, policeman. All you have to do is take my hand on it and it will cost you nothing, nothing at all."

Mazaraki's right hand was stretched out. Rostnikov for the first time stepped back, not wanting to touch or be touched by that hand, as if the touch would give him a disease of thought that he could not overcome, a disease he might welcome. Mazaraki stepped forward, leering now, and Rostnikov's good leg kicked the upturned light, sending out a crack of leather heel on metal, and with the crack Mazaraki stopped, a startled look on his face. He stopped, opened his mouth to speak, and whispered, "Nothing at . . . all."

And then the big man in red fell on his face. In the center of the back of the fallen man's red jacket Rostnikov could see an uneven wet pattern of an even darker red. Rostnikov looked up into the dark arena.

"Katya?" he said.

"Yes," came the woman's voice.

There really wasn't anything else to say. If he had been a younger man with a good leg, Rostnikov could have leaped over the lamp into the protection of darkness, but a leap was out of the question and a shuffling roll would be ludicrous and undignified. He felt the dull heat of the light directly behind his good leg. His weak leg could take no more than a pained instant of weight. He gave it that instant and kicked back at the light with his heel. The glass shattered and the bullet from the darkness hummed past him as he turned to his right and moved as quickly as he could into the darkness. She fired again. Three more shots. All three to Rostnikov's right. And then a pause. The body of Mazaraki lay silently. A thin wisp of smoke rose from the dead lamp, and a shuffling rush of footsteps came closer.

Something moved at the far reaches of the remaining light. He pressed himself against the wall behind him and waited for Katya Rashkovskaya to run across the ring, gun in hand, and find him. "*Nichevo*," he said to himself. If it were to be like this, then it would be like this.

She stepped into the light slowly, her hands at her side. She was dressed in white and, Rostnikov thought, looked quite darkly beautiful. And then someone appeared behind her and then someone else.

"Porfiry!" came Sarah's voice.

And into the light behind Katya Rashkovskaya stepped Sarah and Sasha Tkach. Sasha was holding a gun. Katya was empty-handed.

"I'm all right," Rostnikov said, stepping forward.

"I called," Sarah said, looking down at the dead man.

"I see," said Rostnikov, moving forward toward her.

Sasha pushed his unruly hair from his face and smiled at Rostnikov, who nodded. Katya didn't smile. She looked emotionlessly at Mazaraki's body and leaned over to pick up the red hat.

As Sarah put her head against his chest, Rostnikov wondered if he should wait till morning to retrieve the plumbing books he had loaned to Katya Rashkovskaya.

* * *

Deputy Procurator Khabolov was dreaming about Helsinki, which, even in his sleep, he found quite odd, for he had never been to Helsinki nor did he have any interest in going to Helsinki. He found himself walking the streets of Helsinki certain that he was getting lost, unable to retrace his steps because he did not know where he had begun, unable to ask anyone who passed him for directions because they all spoke to each other in a language that must have been Finnish. Suddenly, behind him, came a pounding noise. In his dream he turned as the noise came closer, became louder, more insistent. Fear pressed him against the brick wall of a building while he waited for the massive ball of iron that pounded toward him, would surely, suddenly, come around a corner to crush him. He looked for help at the Finns around him who did not stop but kept walking, smiling.

"Answer the door," one of the Finns said without moving his mouth, and Khabolov sat up in bed, awake, panting in fear. "The door," his wife repeated. "Someone's at the door."

Khabolov looked at his wife, who had turned her huge freckled back on him and was clutching a pillow to her head.

The knock came again. "Can you dream that people are speaking Finnish if you can't understand Finnish?" he asked.

"Answer the door," his wife replied, and Khabolov pushed back the covers, checked the buttons on his pajamas, smoothed down his hair with two hands, and looked at the clock on the dresser. Six o'clock in the morning. The knock came again, and he padded quickly out of the bedroom and toward the door. The knock came again.

"Who is it?" he called.

"Rostnikov" was the reply.

Khabolov checked himself in the mirror next to the door, didn't like what he saw, and shouted "One moment" as he hurried back to get the blue-and-white and too-warm-for-this-weather flannel robe in the closet. His wife said something half in sleep. He ignored her and closed the bedroom door on his way out.

When he opened the apartment door, Deputy Procurator Khabolov saw that Inspector Rostnikov was not alone. Tkach stood at his side, a bit pale, almost at attention.

"What is it?" Khabolov asked, assuming a terrible emergency. Rostnikov was not even working for the Procurator's Office any longer, and no inspector had ever visited, ever been invited to visit, Khabolov's apartment. Khabolov had no desire for anyone outside of his family and his few friends to see what he had accumulated in appliances and the minor luxuries that made life tolerable.

"May we come in for a moment, Comrade?" Rostnikov asked politely. Both were quite sober and serious, yet neither gave the impression that an emergency was in progress.

"I'd like to know..." Khabolov began and stopped when Rostnikov reached into his pocket and pulled out an oblong package wrapped in a brown paper bag. The object looked like a small book. Khabolov looked at both policemen sternly, discerned nothing, and took the package. He opened it and extracted something he recognized, a videotape.

"What is this?"

"A videotape," Rostnikov said.

Khabolov could see that it was a videotape. For a moment he thought he might still be dreaming. The scene made as much sense as his dream about Helsinki.

"We think," Rostnikov continued, "that you should look at it."

"Now?" Khabolov asked them.

"Now would be a very good time, or you could wait till later," said Rostnikov, letting his eyes focus beyond Khabolov on the interior of the room.

"What is it? Some murder evidence? Inspector Karpo included in his report on the apprehension of the prostitute killer that you had been instrumental in . . . It has nothing to do with that case?"

Rostnikov shook his head no, and Tkach remained at near-attention.

"I'm running out of patience," said Khabolov, bouncing the videotape in his hand as if it were growing warm. "Very well. Come in, but mark you, this had better be important."

Rostnikov and Tkach entered the room, and Khabolov closed the door quietly behind them.

"Come and be quiet. My wife is sleeping in there."

Neither man had known Khabolov had a wife, but that did not surprise or interest them as much as the brown carpeting on the floor. Not a rug in the center of the room, but real carpeting. Sasha Tkach wondered if the apartment had more than one bedroom.

Khabolov led them across the room to a sofa facing a television set with a video machine on a table next to it.

"Better be important," Khabolov warned, turning on his machines and inserting the tape. A static-filled image came on with a flamelike sound and Khabolov plopped on the sofa to watch. He did not invite the two policemen to sit. They stood and watched the screen.

"It had better be important," Khabolov said again. "Murder evidence or—"

"Profiteering," Rostnikov supplied. "Black market, probably. We think it important enough to consider turning over to the KGB. We thought you might be the one to do it."

"I see," said Khabolov, and for an instant he thought he did see. These two wanted to get on his good side. They had stumbled onto something important and had brought it to him. Rostnikov wanted his job back. Tkach wanted some assurance about his security. In exchange they were giving him something he could turn over to the KGB. And then the static stopped and a picture came on the screen. It was a bit dark. The camera jiggled but the picture was clear. There was no mistaking the interior of the Gorgasali trailer. And there were the Gorgasali brothers. Someone said something on the tape. Khabolov couldn't make it out. And then a figure came through the trailer door and Khabolov leaped up from the sofa. He was looking at himself. He plunged his hands into the pockets of the robe and came up with a handkerchief. He threw it at the nearby table and missed. Before the Khabolov in the picture could speak, the Khabolov in the apartment reached over and snapped the television off.

"You are playing a dangerous game, you two," Khabolov said, retrieving the tape from the machine and plunging it into his now-empty pocket.

"You may keep that one," Rostnikov said. "We have another copy."

"Blackmail? You are daring to blackmail me?" Khabolov said, looking at Tkach, who looked at Rostnikov.

"It would appear so," said Rostnikov.

"I'll go to the Chief Procurator, tell him it's a fake, tell him you two are in on this. If I lose my job, you lose yours. If I go to jail, you go. Especially you, Tkach. You were the one who made contact with those two."

Khabolov pointed to the blank television screen to indicate that it held the Gorgasali brothers.

"Perhaps so, perhaps not," Rostnikov said. "The Chief Procurator might believe you. He might not. It might be reasonable to hear our terms before you try to make threats."

"I don't deal with blackmailers," Khabolov said defiantly, but there was no backbone in his defiance. As he spoke, he pulled the sash of the flannel robe tightly around his waist as if he were suddenly cold.

"Then, perhaps, those are the only criminals with whom you do not deal," sighed Rostnikov. "Or at least have not dealt with till now."

"Say what you have to say and then get out," Khabolov said, looking from one man to the other with his sternest glare. It seemed to have no effect. "I'll decide what to do with you."

"The terms are simple," said Rostnikov. "May I sit? My leg . . ."

"Sit, sit, sit, sit," said Khabolov with irritation.

Rostnikov moved to a straight-backed wooden chair against the wall and sat.

"Keep your video machine, the tapes you have," said Rostnikov. "Destroy all records of your dealings with the Gorgasali brothers and never visit them again. No investigation of them was made. Inspector Tkach did not visit them. He did not talk to you about them."

"I'm listening," said Khabolov.

"Good," said Rostnikov. "If Sasha Tkach is mentioned in a report or involved in any way with your dealings in this or any other illegal matter, the tape goes to the Chief Procurator."

"And for yourself, eh?" Khabolov asked, shaking his head. "You want to be transferred back to the Procurator's Office."

"No," said Rostnikov. "You haven't the power to grant such a transfer. The decision was made above you and I have no desire to return. But a request for permanent transfer of Inspectors Tkach and Karpo to MVD investigation under Colonel Snitkonoy may be coming through and we would appreciate your doing your utmost to see to it that it is approved."

"Tkach?" Khabolov snapped.

"I have nothing to add," said Sasha, meeting Khabolov's eyes.

The deputy procurator bounced once on his bare feet and decided that he could live with this. It would be better, under the circumstances, to get rid of Tkach and Karpo, two spies for Rostnikov. Maybe someday in some way he would be able to get the original tape. The terms were ridiculous. They could have had much more, but, Khabolov realized, that was precisely why Rostnikov had asked for no more. It would be very easy to grant this, easy and relatively painless.

"I'll think about this and decide what to do with you two," he said sternly. "Now get out."

"Be quiet out there," his wife shouted from the bedroom. "I've got to get up in an hour."

"Yes, my *krasee'vliy*, my beauty," Khabolov called, and then he turned to the two men.

Rostnikov stood and walked across the room on the silent carpet with Sasha close behind. Khabolov marched ahead of them to open the door. They exited and Khabolov closed the door quietly behind them without another word.

"I think—" Sasha began, but Rostnikov put his finger to his lips to quiet him.

Sasha nodded in understanding and looked at the door. He was tempted to turn around and knock in the hope that Khabolov had his ear pressed to the other side. The two men walked to the stairway and did not speak till they were down the two flights and out onto Zubovsky Boulevard.

"We won," Tkach said softly.

"More or less," Rostnikov agreed with a shrug.

"He won't destroy the Gorgasali file," said Tkach.

"Would you?"

"No," Sasha agreed as they walked. The morning sky was quickly darkening, and rain had been predicted by both the radio and Sasha's mother earlier that morning.

"It gives him the feeling that he has a secret, something with which to hold us at bay," said Rostnikov. "He won't destroy you if it means destroying himself. And besides, in a few weeks, a month, someone might pay a visit some afternoon to the deputy procurator's office or his home and the file on the Gorgasalis might disappear."

Sasha looked at Rostnikov as if seeing a madman for the first time. He was grateful to the chief inspector but this was all very risky, very dangerous, and Rostnikov seemed so matter-of-fact.

At the metro station they parted, going in different directions. Sasha was about to say something, to thank the chief inspector, but Rostnikov slapped Tkach gently on the cheek, grinned warmly but sadly, and walked away.

Twenty minutes later Sasha Tkach was at Petrovka checking his assignment file and deciding where he would take his family that night to celebrate.

* * *

Rostnikov got to the meeting room almost half an hour early, but he did not beat the Gray Wolfhound, whose brown, bemedaled uniform clung to him without a single wrinkle as he stood examining something he had written on the blackboard for the morning meeting.

"Good morning, Comrade Colonel," Rostnikov said, taking his seat.

Colonel Snitkonoy turned, standing erect, hands behind his back, to face the early arrival. On the board behind him Rostnikov could read, written in white chalk, "Surprise, Strength, Strategy," the lesson for the day.

"Early?" the Wolfhound observed without consulting his watch.

"I have a request," said Rostnikov.

"A request," Snitkonoy repeated with a smile, as if he were prepared for whatever surprise, strength, and strategy Rostnikov might display.

"That you consider the possibility of requesting the transfer of two more investigators from the deputy procurator's office," explained Rostnikov.

"Your men?" Snitkonoy asked, beginning to see the ploy.

"In a sense, but only in a sense," agreed Rostnikov. "Two outstanding men who would contribute greatly in their investigative skills to the success of your department."

"My staff size is limited by certain . . . considerations," the Wolfhound said with an eaglelike lifting of his perfect white-maned head.

The size of the staff was limited, Rostnikov knew, by the low esteem in which the Wolfhound was held. His staff was, simply, large enough to make it ceremonial.

"I have reason to believe that, because of certain considerations, the deputy procurator would be most cooperative in such a request," Rostnikov said, looking not at the Wolfhound but at the paper and pencil before him.

"An addition of two experienced investigators to my

staff," Snitkonoy said, looking back at what he had written on the board. "I'll consider it."

Rostnikov reached for the pencil and began to draw.

His back still turned to the chief inspector, the Wolf-hound said, "You had two messages waiting for you this morning. I have taken the liberty of placing them on the tray."

Rostnikov's eyes moved up from the pencil to the tray in the center of the table and found a single sheet of paper with a message neatly printed in the hand of one of the clerks. The time of receipt was early that morning, about the moment he and Tkach had entered Khabolov's apartment. The message read: "Major Zhenya called to inform you that Colonel Drozhkin died during the night. Major Zhenya requests that you come to Lubyanka this morning to discuss with him the unsatisfactory conclusion to the Mazaraki situation."

Rostnikov smiled and plunged the note into his pocket.

Back still turned, the Wolfhound said, "Trouble?"

"A bit," agreed Rostnikov.

The Wolfhound tapped the blackboard with the long piece of chalk in his hand. "Remember, surprise, strength, strategy."

"I'll bear that in mind," Rostnikov said, sketching something that looked like a book.

"I said there were two messages," Snitkonoy reminded him.

"Yes, Colonel."

"Your wife called and asked that one of the clerks tell you that your son will be home on leave in two days." With this Snitkonoy turned abruptly and faced the seated inspector, looking for a change in expression. Rostnikov satisfied him by putting down the pencil and letting the smile lose its sense of irony.

"Thank you, Colonel," Rostnikov said.

"And you say," the Wolfhound asked, tapping his cheek with a long, immaculate finger, "that I can add two men to my staff by simply requesting it?"

"Yes, Colonel."

"Is one of them tall?"

"Yes," said Rostnikov. "Quite tall."

"Good," said the colonel as Pankov came running into the meeting, a look of morning fear on his face. "We can use a bit of height on the staff."

When the Gray Wolfhound's official morning meeting began, Rostnikov's grin showed white, uneven teeth to the puzzled Pankov, who wondered and feared where this morning would end.

For Rostnikov the morning ended a few hours later in Arbat Square. When he entered the metro, the sky had been threatening and dark, with the rumble of thunder from the northwest in the direction of the town of Klin. When he climbed to the square on the steps of the Arbatskaya Metro Station, the rain had already begun, a fine, thin rain with a hint of red in it from the heavy traffic on Suvorov Boulevard. He stood in the shelter of the station next to one of the pillars facing Gogol Boulevard. Beside him a woman hesitated, looked at the dark sky, looked at him, covered her head with a magazine, and dashed toward the nearby Khudozhetvenny Cinema. The sky rumbled and Rostnikov looked toward the statue of the smiling Gogol, about the distance of a soccer field away. He shivered with a sudden slap of cool air and had the uncanny feeling that no time had passed since he had last stood in this same place, in a similar rain, looking toward that statue. He knew he had not dreamed the man on Gogol's head, but at the same time there was the feeling of a dream about the past few days, just as, to a lesser degree, there seemed to be the feeling of a dream to his life, as if he were not within his vulnerable body but an observer who could not be affected by the outside world, could not be affected in spite of the reminder of his leg, which even now throbbed a bit in the dampness, in spite of the vulnerability of the people he knew and touched and who touched him.

The rain eased a bit and Rostnikov left the small group of people who were waiting under the cover of the metro station's roof. He limped slowly to the boulevard, found a break in the traffic, and crossed to the small park in front

of Gogol's statue. The rain was now at that point where
one cannot tell if it is still raining or one is only imagining
it. The street was wet, puddled with reflections of people,
traffic, sky, and it smelled the smell of city he remembered
as a boy. When Josef came in on leave, he would bring him
here, bring him to the sad Gogol a few blocks away in the
courtyard of the building where Gogol had lived. He was
not sure what he would say to Josef when they came, but
he was sure his son would understand.

Rostnikov sighed deeply and looked at the clearing sky.
Morning was over and he could put off no longer his trip to
Lubyanka. Major Zhenya was waiting. If he hurried just a
bit, he knew he could catch the bus that was just turning in
at Arbat Street. As he crossed the street, he was certain
that the rain had now stopped.

ABOUT THE AUTHOR

STUART M. KAMINSKY is the author of three previous Porfiry Rostnikov mysteries: DEATH OF A DISSIDENT, BLACK KNIGHT IN RED SQUARE (an Edgar nominee), and RED CHAMELEON, which the *Chicago Sun-Times* called "a must-read mystery." He is also the author of the highly acclaimed Toby Peters mystery series. He now teaches film history, criticism, and production at Northwestern University, where he is a professor and head of the Division of Film. He lives in Skokie, Illinois, with his wife and three children.